This Wicked Gift

D1607983

COURTNEY MILAN

This is a work of fiction. Names, characters, places, and incidents are the product of the author's imagination or are used fictitiously. Any resemblance to actual events, locales, or persons, living or dead, is purely coincidental

This Wicked Gift: © 2009 by Courtney Milan.

Cover design © Courtney Milan.

Cover photographs © Anteromite, Subbotina Anna, Malyugin, and manifeesto | shutterstock.com.

Print Edition 2.0

For Mass-yo (with a dash), the best little brother that staged protests and hunger strikes can buy. We wanted to do everything for you, and you were too smart to let us.

P.S. You know that thing with the face, shoes, Germany? Sorry about that. But can you stop mentioning it every time we see each other?

Chapter One

London, 1822

IT WAS FOUR DAYS until Christmas and four minutes until the family lending library closed for the evening. Lavinia Spencer sat, the daily ledger opened on the desk in front of her, and waited for the moment when the day would end and she could officially remove her five pennies from the take. Every day since summer, she'd set aside a coin or five from her family's earnings. She'd saved the largesse in a cloth bag in the desk drawer, where nobody would find it and be tempted to spend it. Over the weeks, her bag had begun to burgeon. Now, she had almost two pounds.

Two pounds in small, cold coins to the rest of the world. For Lavinia, the money meant pies. Spices, sugar and wine to mull them with. And, once she scoured the markets, perhaps a goose—a small goose—roasted alongside their usual turnips. Her two pounds meant a Christmas celebration that would make Papa sit up and smile. Six months of planning—but the effort had been worth it, because Lavinia was going to deliver a holiday meal just like the ones her mother had prepared.

The business they'd conducted today had been frenetic. Lavinia finished adding columns in the daybook and nodded to herself. Today's take—according to her records—had been very fine indeed. If she hadn't miscalculated, today she'd let herself take *six* pennies from the till—half a shilling that made her that much more certain of goose, as opposed to mere stewing fowl. Lavinia took a deep breath. Layered atop the musk of leather-bound volumes and India ink, she could almost detect the scent of roast poultry. She imagined the red of mulled wine swirling in mugs. And in her mind's eye, she saw her father sitting taller in his chair, color finally touching his cheeks.

She reached for the cash box and started counting.

The bell above the door rang—at a minute to closing. A gust of winter wind poured in. Lavinia looked up, prepared to be annoyed. But when she saw who had entered, she caught her breath.

It was *him*. Mr. William Q. White—and what the Q stood for, she'd not had the foresight to demand on the day when he'd purchased his subscription. But the name rolled off the tongue. *William Q. White*. She could never think of him as simply a monosyllabic last name. His name had rolled off her tongue, as it happened, far too many times in the last year for her own good.

He took off his hat and gloves at the threshold and shook droplets of water from the sodden gray of his coat. Mr. William Q. White was tall and his dark hair was cropped close to his skull. He did not dawdle in the doorway, letting the rain into the shop as so many other customers did. Instead, he moved quickly, purposefully, without ever appearing to rush. It was not even a second before he closed the door on the frigid winter and entered the room. Despite his alacrity, he did not track in mud.

His eyes, a rich mahogany, met hers. She bit her lip and twisted her feet around the legs of her stool. He spoke little, but what he said—

"Miss Spencer." He gestured with his hat in acknowledgment.

Unremarkable words, but her toes curled in their slippers nonetheless. He spoke in a deep baritone, his voice as rich as the finest drinking chocolate. But what really made her palms tingle was a wild, indefinable *something* about his accent. It wasn't the grating Cockney the delivery boys employed, nor the flat, pompous perfection of the London aristocracy. He had a pure, cultured voice—but one that was nonetheless from somewhere many miles distant. His Rs had just a hint of a roll to them; his vowels stretched and elongated into elegant diphthongs. Every time he said "Miss Spencer," the exotic cadence of his speech seemed to whisper, "I have been places."

She imagined him adding, "Would you like to come with me?"

Yes. Yes, she would. Lavinia rather fancied a man with long…vowels.

And oh, she knew she was being foolish and giddy about Mr. William Q. White. But if a girl couldn't be foolish and giddy about a man when she was nineteen, when *could* she be foolish? It was hard to be serious all the time, especially when there was so much to be serious about.

And so she took a risk. "Merry Christmas, Mr. White."

He was examining the shelves. At her words, he turned toward her. His eyes slid from her waist up to her face, and Lavinia ducked her head and stared at the stack of pennies in front of her to hide her blush.

He didn't need to speak to make her giddy, not when he looked at her with that breathtaking intensity. For one scalding moment, she thought he was going to address her. He might even step toward her. Her hands curled around the edge of the desk in anticipation. But instead, he shook his head and turned back to the shelves.

A pity. Not today, then. Maybe not any day. And with Mr. William Q. White ignoring her again, it was time for Lavinia to set her fancies to one side and give herself over to seriousness. She counted the coins from the cash box and piled them into stacks of twelve, making sure to exactly align the pennies atop each other before starting a new pile.

Lavinia prided herself on her ability to get the take exactly right. Her longest stretch of perfection was thirty-seven days in a row, spanning the entirety of October. That run had been ruined by a penny's difference on November 4. She had no intention of letting October's record stand, however. It had been twenty-two days since her last error. Today would be number twenty-three.

She'd counted and double-counted every transaction. If she was so much as a ha'penny short, she'd eat Mr. William Q. White's extremely wet hat. Her hands flew as she placed dirty coins into careful piles. Four, six, eight, and with the loose coins, that made seven shillings, and four and one-halfpence. Less than she'd imagined. She bit her lip in suspicion and glanced at the tally in the ledger.

Trepidation settled in an indigestible mass in Lavinia's belly. There, written in black and white in the daily ledger, was the final sum. Ten shillings, four and one-half pence.

She wasn't half a penny short. She was missing three full shillings.

Lavinia recounted the coins, but there was no error. Of course not; Lavinia did not make errors in accounting. Nobody would take her to task for the missing coins. Her father was too ill to examine the books, and her brother would never question Lavinia's jurisdiction over the shop.

Still, she did not like to question herself. How had she made such a stupendous error? She felt a touch of vertigo, as if the room were spinning in circles around the ledger.

She knew what she had to do. It hurt—oh, how it stung. Those three shillings could be the difference between a small goose and no goose at all. But with her father's creditors clamoring, and the cost of his medicines growing almost monthly, the family could not spare more than a handful of pennies' loss each day. Lavinia slid open the drawer to make up the difference from her precious Christmas hoard.

She always placed the bag in the same spot—precisely halfway back and flush against the left side. But her fingers met no velvet mass lumpy with coin. She groped wildly and found nothing but the smooth wood of the drawer from corner to corner. Lavinia held her breath and peered inside. There was nothing in the drawer but a cracked inkwell, and that—she checked—contained nothing but bluish smears.

"Hell." It was the worst curse word she could imagine. She whispered it; it was either that, or shriek.

She wasn't missing a few shillings. She was missing the full two pounds. All of Christmas had just disappeared—everything from the decoration holly down through her carefully planned menu.

"Vinny?" The words were a tremulous query behind her.

With those words, the rising tide of Lavinia's panic broke against an absolute certainty. She knew where her precious two pounds had gone.

Lavinia placed her hands on her hips. She forced herself to turn around slowly, rather than whirling as she wished. Her brother, still wrapped for the blustery weather outside, smiled weakly, holding out his hands in supplication. Water dripped from his coat and puddled on the floor.

James was four years younger than her, but Mama had always said to subtract ten years from a man's age when calculating his sense. James had never seen fit to prove Mama's formula wrong.

"Oh." He peered beyond her to the coins, stacked in grim military ranks along the edge of the counter and the ransacked drawer. His lip quirked. "I see you've, um, already tallied the cash."

"James Allen Spencer." Lavinia reached out and grabbed his ear.

He winced, but didn't dodge or protest—a sure sign of guilt.

"What," she demanded, "have you done with my two pounds?"

⌘ ⌘ ⌘

IT WAS WARM inside the lending library, but William White still felt cold inside. His hand clenched around the solitary bank note in his pocket. The paper crumpled in his fist, cutting into his palm. It had been ten years since anyone had wished him a merry Christmas. Fitting, that it would happen on this day— and that Lavinia Spencer would be the one to do so.

Christmas was a luxury for the wealthy—or, perhaps, an illusion for the young and innocent. William had not been any of those since the winter evening a decade ago when he'd been cut off from the comfortable life he'd been living.

He stared past the books shelved in front of him, their titles blurring with the smooth leather of their bindings. The scene clouded into an indistinct, foggy mass.

Tonight, a solicitor had finally tracked him down. William had been leaving his master's counting house, having just finished another pitiful day of pitiful work, performed for the pitiful salary of four pounds ten a quarter. As soon as he'd set foot outside, he'd been set upon by an unctuous man.

For one second, when the lawyer had introduced himself, a flush of uncharacteristic optimism had swept through William. Mr. Sherrod had seen fit to remember the promise he'd made. William could come home. He could forget the menial work he did as a clerk. He could abandon the grim day-to-day existence of labor followed by sleep and bone-chilling want.

But no. It turned out Adam Sherrod was not unctuous. He was dead.

He'd remembered William in his will—to the tune of ten pounds. Ten pounds, when he'd been responsible for the loss of William's comfort, his childhood and, ultimately, William's father. Ten pounds, when he had promised most sincerely to take care of William, should it be necessary. It had become necessary ten Christmases ago, and Mr. Sherrod had not lifted a finger to help.

William had no real claim on Mr. Sherrod's money. He had, in fact, nothing but the memory of a promise that the man had kicked to one side. But still, he'd remembered.

Thus dissipated one of the elaborate dreams he'd fashioned to motivate himself on the hardest days. He would never return to Leicester. He would never be able to rise above his father's errors; hell, he would never even rise above his fellow clerks. This evening, he'd been damned to live in the hell of poverty for the rest of his life. There would be no salvation.

That last legacy should have been no surprise. After all, it was only in fairy tales that Dick Whittington came to London as an impoverished lad and ended up Lord Mayor. In reality, a man counted himself lucky to earn eighteen pounds a year.

So yes, Christmas was for the young. It was for blue-eyed angels like Miss Lavinia Spencer, who would never be confronted with the true ugliness of life. It was for women who wished customers a merry Christmas without imagining the holiday could be anything other than happy. Christmas was not for men who'd had one of two fantasies shattered in one evening.

It was the second fantasy that had drawn William here.

Miss Spencer was slim and vivacious. She couldn't help but move her hands when she talked. She smiled far too much. She blushed far too easily. And her hair was forever falling out of its pins into unruly cinnamon waves that clung to her neck. She was one of those souls who remembered countless trivialities—names of customers, names of cats, the health of everyone's spouse.

If he'd received even a fraction of those ten thousand pounds, as promised… Well, that was a subject for many a cold and lonely night indeed.

Because he'd have found a way to get her into his bed, over and over.

William paused, his hand on the spine of a book, and attempted to banish the image that heated thought conjured. Miss Lavinia Spencer, undoing the ties that fastened her cloak. The wool would fall to the floor in a swirl, and those cinnamon waves of hair would slip from their pins. He couldn't think of that. Not now. Not here. It was not, however, his strength of mind that sent the vision away. It was the sound of speech.

"Vinny, you have to understand." The recalcitrant whine of her brother was barely audible from where William stood, obscured by the shelves.

Over the past year, the elder Mr. Spencer had come into the shop less frequently. William had noted with some disapproval that it was Miss Spencer who'd taken his place downstairs. She'd greeted customers and accepted deliveries. Her brother, James, had been conspicuously absent from useful employment.

"It was just a temporary loan. He needed the money to pay the guards so he could get at his goods without his creditors finding out." James ended on a querulous note, as if his bald assertion yearned to become a question.

"*Bribe* the guards, you mean." That was Miss Spencer—incorruptible, of course. She was speaking in an almost whisper, but the shop was quiet enough that William could hear every word echoing amongst the books.

"But Mr. Cross promised me ten percent! And he even drew up a proper partnership agreement. Since you never let me help in here, I thought I could find a way to pay Papa's bills on my own. I was going to buy you a Christmas present. When's the last time you had a new dress, Vinny?"

"I'd rather have my two pounds. You *are* getting to the part where you took the money without asking me?"

"I thought I'd be able to slip it back in before you found out. After all, Mr. Cross's warehouse was supposed to contain three hundred bricks of tea, and several casks of indigo. Ten percent would have been a fortune."

There was a moment of disapproving silence. "I see. Since you do not seem to be weighed down by exorbitant shipping profits, I must conclude your foray into trade was unsuccessful."

A sullen scuffle of shoes followed. "After I gave him the two pounds, Cross told me we needed fifty more to pay the excise men."

"I see."

William had heard of similar tricks before. It was the sort of fraudulent promise made by ruffians who preyed on the greedy and the indolent—a pledge of fabulous wealth, soon, if only the mark in question handed over a tiny amount. It started with a few shillings. Next, the trickster would require three pounds for a bribe, followed by fifty for customs. The fraud only ended when the target was bled dry.

"Well, of course I saw through him *then,*" the younger Spencer continued. "I called him a cheat. And then he told me he'd have me up in front of a magistrate for failing to deliver on my promissory note."

"Your *what?*"

"Uh." James drew the syllable out. His hesitance echoed among the books. "You recall that partnership agreement?"

"Yes…?" She did not sound the least bit encouraging.

"It turns out that paper I signed was actually a promissory note for ten pounds."

The inarticulate cry of protest Miss Spencer made was not angelic at all. William peeked around the corner. She was seated on her stool, her head in her hands. She rocked back and forth, the seat tipping precariously. Finally she spoke through her fingers. "You didn't *read* it when you signed it?"

"He looked honest."

Wood scraped against the slate floor as Miss Spencer pushed her stool back and stood. William pulled his head behind the shelves before she could spot him.

"Oh, my Lord," she swore, downright unrighteous in her wrath. "A man offered you a partnership predicated upon attempted bribery, and you didn't question his integrity?"

"Um. No?"

William did not dare breathe into the silence that followed. Then James spoke again. "Vinny, if I must appear before a magistrate, could we claim—"

"Be quiet," she snapped furiously. "I'm thinking."

So was William. Frauds and cheats, if they were any good, made excessively good barristers for themselves in court. The common person could not risk a loss at law. William would not want to stand in young James's shoes before a magistrate. He gave it even odds the boy would prevail.

"No," Miss Spencer said, almost as if she'd heard William's thoughts, and decided to correct him. "We'd win, but we'd have to pay a barrister. No magistrate."

"Vinny, do we have ten pounds? Can't we make him just go away?"

"Not if we want to pay the apothecary."

There was a bleak silence. Likely, Miss Spencer had forgotten William was in the room. If he were a gentleman, he'd have apologized minutes ago and taken his leave.

"We are not without options," Miss Spencer said.

Options. William had a fair idea just how many options Miss Spencer had. He suspected the number was equal to the population of single men who frequented the library—and perhaps included the married ones as well. As the reading men of London were, by definition, neither blind nor completely idiotic, he knew there were many others who entertained charged fantasies about Miss Spencer. In fact, he rather suspected that old Mr. Bellows, the wealthy butcher, would offer her marriage if she gave him the slightest encouragement. Ten pounds would be nothing to him—and the butcher was hardly alone in his lust.

William could not countenance the thought. He could not envision her beneath that fat, toothless man. And besides, the upright Miss Spencer chided her brother about bribery and petty theft. She would never stray from a husband, no matter how many teeth the man lost. If she married, William would never be able to pretend—not even on the darkest, loneliest nights—that he would one day have her.

He'd had enough dreams shattered today.

"I have a plan." There was steel in Miss Spencer's voice. "I'll take care of it."

"What must I do?" James asked instantly.

Miss Spencer was silent. "I think," she said quietly, "you've done enough for now. I'll take care of it for you. Just give me his direction."

Silence stretched, ungracious in its length. Finally her brother heaved a sigh. "Very well. Thank you, Vinny."

Like the foolish coward that he was, her brother complied. William could hear the scratch of pen against paper. James hadn't even asked her what her plan entailed, or insisted that he take care of the matter himself. He didn't care what she might have to sacrifice for him.

William's fists clenched around the bank note in his pocket. If he were a gentleman, he'd hand Miss Spencer his ten pounds and solve all her problems.

Then again, William hadn't been a gentleman since he was fourteen.

No. His ten pounds—his last, minuscule legacy from childhood—would buy him the one fantasy he had left. If she had to sacrifice herself, it might as well be in his honor. She'd wished him a merry Christmas.

Well, she was going to give him one.

⌘   ⌘   ⌘

THE ADDRESS HER BROTHER had inked was still damp on the page when Lavinia's reverie was interrupted.

"He calls you Vinny?"

She looked up and felt her cheeks flush. It was Mr. William Q. White, leaning against the shelves. Of all the people to intrude at this moment. She'd thought the conversation had been quiet. She'd thought him safely ensconced back in the finance section, behind five shelves of books. Obviously she'd been wrong on both counts.

How much had he overheard? How embarrassed ought she to be at playing out that ridiculous drama in front of this serious man? Had she said anything stupid? And how absurd was it that, despite all that had transpired in the last half hour, her heart raced in pitter-patters because Mr. William Q. White had actually *started* a conversation with her?

As she always did when she was nervous, she began to babble. "Yes, he calls me Vinny. It's a pet name for—"

"I know your Christian name, Miss Spencer." His gaze did not move from hers. Instead, he walked across the room to her and stepped behind the counter. He stood too close. If she'd been sitting in a regular chair, she'd have had to crane her neck. Seated on a stool, her feet swinging well above the ground, she still had to lean her head back to look him in the eyes.

He smiled at her, a long, slow grin. In giddy excitement her stomach turned over. That dangerous curve of his lips was a new expression for him. *Assuredly* new. She would have remembered another one like it. Lavinia swallowed.

He set his hand deliberately atop hers.

Oh, she knew she should pull away. Pull away, and slap him for taking liberties with her person. But her brother had left her so cold—and his hand was so warm—and by all that was holy, after a year of encouraging Mr. William Q. White to do more than just look at her, she was not about to raise objections to a little liberty.

"I know what *Vinny* is short for. As it happens, I prefer Lavinia." He leaned over her.

He said it as if he preferred *her*, not just her name. Lavinia's lungs seized. She could smell the starch of his cravat. *He's going to kiss me*, she thought.

Her nipples pressed, painfully peaked, against her stays. His thumb ran along her wrist, down the curve of her fingers. Lavinia felt her lips part. She might even have arched up toward him, just a little. She focused on the pink of his mouth, so close to hers.

He's going to kiss me, and I am going to let him.

Instead, he released her hand. She could still feel the imprint of his fingers against hers as he stepped away.

"Miss Spencer, I do believe we'll talk tomorrow." He smiled. Before she could point out that tomorrow was Sunday, and the lending library would therefore be closed, he tipped his hat at her and set it on his head. "Come find me at one."

And then Mr. William Q. White strode away, the tails of his coat flapping at her. The bell jingled. The door shut. Lavinia raised her burning hand to her unkissed lips and looked down.

It was only then she realized he hadn't been angling for a kiss at all.

He'd taken the slip of foolscap containing the address of the man who'd cheated James.

Chapter Two

LAVINIA WOKE TO A CLOUD of thick, choking smoke. Her first panicked thought was that the books downstairs had somehow caught fire, that their livelihood, half owned by creditors, was going up in flames. But then her conscious mind caught up to her racing fears and she correctly cataloged the smell.

It was the more mundane—and rather more unpleasant—scent of burning porridge.

Frowning, Lavinia pulled a wrapper over her nightdress and padded out into the front room.

James, his hands blackened with soot, was juggling a pot. The vessel let off billows of gray smoke, its sides streaked black.

"Ah," he said essaying a weak smile. "Lavinia! I made breakfast for you."

She didn't dare respond, not even with so little as a raised eyebrow.

He peered into the pot, frowning. "There's still some white bits in here. Isn't it odd that porridge turns *yellow* when it burns? I'd have thought it would go directly to black." He prodded the mass with a spoon, then shrugged and looked up. "Want some?"

Over fifteen years, Lavinia had become quite fluent in the foreign tongue known as Younger Brother. It was a tricky language, mostly because it employed words and phrases that sounded, deceptively, as if they were proper English.

For instance, the average woman off the street would have thought that James had just offered her burned porridge. Lavinia knew better. What James had *actually* said was, "Sorry I stole your money. I made you breakfast by way of apology. Forgive me?"

Lavinia sighed and waved her hand. "Give me a bowl."

That was Younger Brother for: "Your porridge is disgusting, but I love you nonetheless."

By unspoken consensus, as they prepared a tray to bring to their father in bed, James cut a slice of bread and Lavinia slipped it on a toasting fork. Ill as their father was, there was no need to punish him with either the details of James's transgression or an indigestible breakfast.

And perhaps, Lavinia thought as she choked down the nauseating glutinous mass, that was the essence of love. Love wasn't about reasons. It wasn't about admiring fine qualities. Love was a language all on its own, composed of gestures that seemed incomprehensible, perhaps even pointless, to the outside observer.

Speaking of the inarticulate language of love, what had Mr. William Q. White meant by his outrageous behavior last night? *Come find me,* he'd said. His words had seemed to come straight from her imagination.

But surely he hadn't meant for her to look up the address he'd given when he applied for a subscription? Surely he didn't mean she should pay him a visit? A woman who intended to keep her virtue did not visit a man, even if he did have lovely eyes and a voice that spoke of dark seduction. *Especially* if he had those features. Lavinia had gone nineteen years without making any errors at all on that front.

As it happens, I prefer Lavinia. Come find me.

She didn't need to remember the heat of his gaze as he looked at her to know he hadn't asked her to pay an innocent little morning call.

And yet what had her streak of perfection gotten her? Months and months of painstaking taillen had done her no good. Her coins were gone and the very thought of the barren holiday that awaited her family made her palms grow cold.

This somewhat dubious rationale brought Lavinia to the dark, imposing door of 12 Norwich Court. It was not quite an hour after noon, but a dark gray cloud hovered over the tall, bulky houses and blocked all hint of the feeble sun. A wild wind whipped down the street, carrying with it the last few tired leaves from some faraway square and the earthy scent of winter mold. Lavinia pulled her cloak about her in the gloom.

This residential street—little more than a dingy alley, really—was occupied at present only by an orange cat. The animal was a solitary spot of color against the gray-streaked buildings. In the next hour, Lavinia's life could change. Completely. Before she could reconsider, she rapped the knocker firmly against the door. She could feel the blood pounding in her wrists.

And then she waited. She'd almost convinced herself there was nothing unsafe or untoward about this visit. According to the subscription card, Mr. William Q. White had a room on the second floor of a house owned by Mrs. Jane Entwhistle—a cheerful, elderly widow who sometimes visited the lending library in search of gothic novels. Mrs. Entwhistle would doubtless be willing to play chaperone at Lavinia's request. She might even be kindhearted enough to look the other way.

The door opened.

"Oh, Mrs. Entwhistle," Lavinia started. And then she stopped.

It was not the bustling widow who'd opened the door, nor Mary Lee Evans, the scullery maid who was the object of Mrs. Entwhistle's complaints.

Behind the threshold, Mr. William Q. White stood in his shirtsleeves. He was in a shocking state of dishabille. Beneath that single layer of rough white linen, Lavinia could make out the broad line of his shoulders, and the sleek curve of muscles. His cuffs had been folded up, and she could see fine lines of hair at his wrist. She peeped behind him. Surely the respectable Mrs. Entwhistle wouldn't countenance such laxity of dress.

The widow was nowhere to be seen.

She glanced down the street. The cat sat, licking its paws, on a step three houses down.

"Mrs. Entwhistle is gone for the week to celebrate Christmas with her granddaughter." He raised his gaze to her. She ought to have felt cold; his every word came out in a puff of white in the chilled air. But his eyes were hot, and suddenly, so was Lavinia.

"Mary Lee?" she asked in a squeak.

"Given the week off. Come in before you catch your death."

Her imagination gave those words a wicked quality—as if he'd asked her to catch something else instead. It was that accent again, that lilt in his voice that she just couldn't place. It made her think of unspeakable things, no matter how innocent his intentions.

But no, it was not just her imagination. It was a terribly wicked notion to enter a home alone with a young, attractive—very attractive—partially clothed man. Why, he might take liberties. He might take lots of them.

He smiled at her, a mischievous grin that unfolded across his face. Maybe it was her imagination again, but the smile didn't reach his eyes.

"I can't come in. It wouldn't be proper."

"I give you my word," he said carefully, "that I shall not do anything to you without your permission."

As reassurances went, this lacked some basic quality of…assurance.

"Your word as a gentleman?"

His lip curled slightly. "I'm hardly that."

Well, then. "What do you mean, without my permission? I could easily give permission to—"

She stopped herself before she could complete the sentence. Not only because she was embarrassed by her unintended admission, but because if she started cataloging the things she might let him do, given the proper persuasion, she would never stop with a mere peck on the cheek. He was a mere twelve inches from her, on the threshold. She could see him complete her sentence. His pupils dilated. His gaze slipped down her body, a caress that was almost palpable. His Adam's apple bobbed, once.

Still he didn't say anything. It was one thing to have him look the other way when she wished him a merry Christmas, or asked him what he'd thought of the Adam Smith he returned. It was quite another to admit she wanted a kiss, and to have him remain silent.

"Say something," Lavinia begged. "Say anything."

He moved closer. "Come inside with me." His voice enfolded her like warm velvet. And still he looked at her, those dark eyes boring into her, then settling against her lips like a caress.

No. She was past the point of fooling herself. Whatever Mr. William Q. White had done with the address, she had little doubt that if she followed him inside, she would likely be kissed quite thoroughly indeed. She'd known it all along. Perhaps, even, that was why she'd come. And this time he'd said aloud what she'd always imagined. *Come inside with me.*

He was going to kiss her. There was nobody about to see her lapse. Even the cat had disappeared. It was nearly Christmas, and Lavinia didn't suppose she would get any other gift this year. She was cold, and his breath was warm.

She untied her bonnet strings and followed him inside.

The entry was cold and dark and empty, and Mr. White didn't even stop to take her things. Instead, he hustled her up two flights of stairs. The halls of the second landing lacked the soft, feminine furnishings that Mrs. Entwhistle employed downstairs. Instead, they had a Spartan, military look. The walls were the stark yellow of age-faded whitewash.

Mr. White glanced at her, his lips pressed together, and then turned down a silent hall into a back room. The furniture was austere wood. From ceiling to baseboard, there was not even a hint of color on the unadorned walls. A white washstand bore a white pitcher and—a sign that she was in territory that was undeniably masculine—a black-handled razor. A single window looked out over a desolate, gray yard. A solitary tree, stripped to its bare branches by winter, huddled sullenly in the center.

And Lavinia was looking everywhere but in the corner, where there was a bed. It was as cold and forbidding as the rest of the room, made perfectly, without the smallest wrinkle in the white linens.

A bed. This visit was becoming most improper indeed.

Mr. White pulled up a chair—the lone chair in the room, a straight-backed wooden affair—for Lavinia. She sat.

He walked over to a small table and picked up a piece of paper.

"I've purchased your brother's promissory note," he said stiffly.

She hadn't quite known what to expect. "I hope you didn't pay the full ten pounds for it," she said. "Why would you do such a thing?"

He sat on the bed and fiddled with his rolled-up cuffs. She could see the blue lines of veins in his wrist. His fingers were quite long, and Lavinia could imagine them touching her cheek, a gentle tap-tap, in tune with the ditty he beat on his palm now. She wondered whether Mrs. Entwhistle often visited relatives, and if so, whether Mr. White regularly entertained women in his quarters.

But no. He was far too ill at ease. A practiced seducer would have plied her with brandy. He would have made her laugh. Certainly he would not have made her sit in this hard and uncomfortable chair. And he would not have said so little.

"Why do you suppose," he said, "I've asked to talk with you rather than your brother?"

"Because I'm more reasonable than him?"

"Because," he said uneasily, not quite meeting her eyes, "*you*—or rather, your body—is the only currency that can persuade me to part with that note."

It took her a second to unravel his meaning. He wasn't hoping for a kiss given out of gratitude. He wasn't even going to attempt a somewhat awkward seduction. Instead, he was trying to *coerce* her. There had been something magical about the looks he'd given her, occluded as they'd been with his two-word greetings. She'd felt as if they were uncovering a mutual secret—a world where Lavinia could forget the strain of trying to hold her family together. She could pretend for just one instant that nothing mattered but that she was a young woman, desired by an attractive young man.

But her own wishes were of no importance to him. If he was trying to force her in this ridiculous fashion, he saw nothing mutual at all about their desire. She had the sudden feeling of vertigo, as if the room were spinning about her, the floor very far away. As if she'd added all the lines in the ledger between them, and found that her tally did not match his coins.

Lavinia folded her arms about her for warmth.

"Mr. William Q. White," she said calmly. "You are a despicable blackguard."

⌘ ⌘ ⌘

WILLIAM KNEW HE WAS a despicable blackguard. Only the worst of fellows would have tried to claim a woman he could not marry. But he wanted her enough that he almost didn't care.

"I suppose you think I should forgive your brother's debt," William heard himself say.

"I do."

"And what would I stand to gain by that?"

She dropped her eyes. "He is not yet twenty-one, you see."

As if such a fact would have swayed him. Her brother was older than fourteen, and at that age William had first become responsible for his own care. Since then, he'd labored for every scrap of comfort. He'd had nothing handed to him—not a penny, not a kind word, and certainly not a sister who shielded him from every discomfort.

"You will soon learn," he said, more harshly than he'd intended, "that everything has a cost." Coal and blankets in grim lodging houses cost pennies. The eye-straining labor of his apprenticeship had cost him his youth. For years, he'd spent his late nights reading business and agriculture by the dim red glow of the fire, not for pleasure or enjoyment, but to keep alive the futile dream that one day he would be asked to take his place managing funds that might have belonged to him. Mr. Sherrod's will had just stolen that dream from him, too. Oh, yes, William knew everything about cost.

Her color heightened. If he were the sort to engage in self-delusion, he'd imagine that the pink flush on her cheeks was desire. But the breaths that lifted her bosom had to be fear. Fear at his proximity.

Fear that a man, intent and closeted alone with her, was looking down at her with such intensity.

But she did not shrink back, not even when he stood and walked toward her. She didn't falter when he stopped inches from her. She did not quail when he towered over her and peered into the pure blue of her eyes.

Instead, she huffed. "You have not taken my meaning. It is surely in your best interests to collect on the debt owed over time. After all…"

Her voice was husky. Her breath whispered against his lips. He inhaled. Her scent coiled in his veins and joined the throbbing pulse of blood through his body.

"My interest?" His voice was quiet. "I assure you, my only interest is in your body."

Her eyes widened. Her lips parted. And that long, smooth column of throat contracted in a swallow.

And then, inexplicable woman that she was, Lavinia smiled. "You're not very good at this, are you? It works better if you give your villainy at least a thin veneer of pleasantry."

He might have been a blackguard, but he had no intention of being a liar. "Nothing really worth having is free. If the cost of having you is your hatred, I'll pay it."

She didn't shrink from him. Instead, she tilted her head, as if seeing him at an angle would change his requirements. The pulse in her throat beat rapidly—one, two, three, he counted, all the way up to twenty-two, before she raised her chin.

"Am I worth having, then? At this cost to yourself?"

"You're worth ten pounds." It was heresy to say those words, heresy to place so low a value on her. It was heresy even to think of someone as low as him touching a woman as incomparable as her. But he was going to be in hell all his life. He wanted one memory, one dream to keep with him in the years of drudgery that would surely follow. He'd have traded his soul to the devil to have her. A little heresy would hardly signify.

She stood. On her feet, she was mere inches from him. "You believe," she said, her voice unsteady, "that you must *purchase* the best things in life. With bank notes."

"I have no other currency to barter with."

She met his eyes. "Is there anything you want in addition to my body? That is—will once be enough, or will this turn into a...a regular occurrence?"

A regular occurrence. His body tensed at the thought. He wanted everything about her. Her smile, when she saw him; her sudden laughter, breaking like a sunrise in the night of his life. He wanted her, over and over, body and soul and spirit. But that was all well out of his price range. And so he asked for the one thing he thought he might get.

"I want one other thing," he said. "When I touch you, I want you not to flinch."

She frowned in puzzlement at this proclamation. As she bit her lip, she reached for the catch of her cloak. She fumbled with the ties, and then removed the wool from her shoulders, folding the cloth into a careful square. The dress underneath was a faded rose, the fabric old enough that it had shaped itself to the curves of her hips. He'd seen her in the gown before, but never while he stood close enough to touch.

She tugged on her left glove, loosening each finger before rolling the material down her arm. He noted, with some distraction, that there was a tiny hole in the index finger. Her fingers seemed impossibly slender.

"Very well," she said. "I agree."

He hadn't really believed it would happen. He had passed last night, after he'd retrieved her brother's note of promise, in a delirium of dazzled lust. But up until this moment, he'd expected her to walk away, snatched from him like all his other dreams. She removed her second glove, as slowly as she'd taken off the first, and aligned the two precisely before setting them atop her cloak. He swallowed. When she slid the pins from her hair, letting that coiled mass of cinnamon spill down her back, he realized he was really going to have her. Somehow, this impossible plan had worked.

If he were a gentleman, he'd stop now and send her on her way.

She turned her back to him—not, he realized, to hide her face. No, Lavinia didn't shrink from him.

Instead, she lifted the mass of her hair so that he could unlace her dress.

The gesture gave him a perfect view of the back of her neck. It was slim and long. He could make out the delicate swells of her spine. Up until this point, nothing truly untoward had happened, except in William's mind. But once he touched her—once he unlaced that gown—it would be too late for them both. If he had any strength of character at all, he'd leave her untouched. But all his strength had turned into pounding blood, thundering through his veins. And if he had any will at all, it was directed toward this—this moment of heaven, stolen from the angel who had haunted his dreams for a year.

He would never find forgiveness if he took her, but then he'd been damned for a decade. All he would ever know of paradise was Lavinia. And so he laid his hands on her waist and claimed his damnation.

She was warm against his palms, and oh, it had been so long since he touched another human being. He leaned in and kissed the back of her neck. She tasted of lemon soap. His arms wrapped around her, drawing her against his body. She nestled against his erection, and by God, she did what he'd asked. She didn't flinch. Instead, she sighed and leaned back into his arms, as if she enjoyed the feel of his touch.

"Miss Spencer," he murmured in her ear.

"You'd better call me Lavinia."

His fingers found the ties of her dress and unraveled them carefully. Then he slid the dress off her shoulders. Long muslin sleeves fell away to reveal creamy shoulders, milk-white arms. When the gown hit the floor, she turned in his arms. She was wearing nothing but stays and a chemise. Her skin was warm against his hands and she arched up toward him. Her lips parted. Her eyes shone at him, as if he were her lover instead of the man who'd forced her into this. She'd looked at him that way, just last night in the library. Surely, then, she hadn't meant to invite a kiss.

He was not such a fool as to turn down that invitation twice. He kissed her, hard, savoring the feel of her lips against his. She tasted as sweet as a glass of water after a hard day's labor, felt as welcome as sunshine in the darkness of winter. He pulled her into his embrace roughly. She twitched in surprise when his tongue touched her lips, but she opened her mouth with an eagerness that made up for any apparent inexperience.

He had to remind himself that she'd not chosen this, that he'd ordered her not to flinch from his advances. It was not real, the way she nestled in his arms. It was not real, the way her hands pressed against his back, pulling his thighs against hers. It was not real, the way she opened up to him. It was all a fraud, obtained through coercion.

He was impoverished enough that he'd take her caresses anyway.

She pulled away from him, but only to unlace her stays. As she lifted her arms above her head, a stray shaft of light came through the window and illuminated the outline of her legs through her chemise. She let her stays drop to the ground. She didn't look up—no doubt suddenly ashamed, aware that William could make out the dusky purple of her areolae through her chemise. A shaft of heat rippled through William, and he could wait no longer.

Without thinking, he walked forward. His hands slid up her waist. She was separated from him by the thinnest layer of cloth. She shivered as he drew her toward him. And then he leaned forward and closed his mouth around the dusky tip of her nipple. Even through her chemise, he could feel it contract, pebbling under his tongue.

"Oh!" Her hand clutched his arm spontaneously.

He licked that hard tip, as if somehow, her response would count as real acquiescence. Maybe, if he was good enough to her, if he brought her to the most trembling peak of pleasure, she would forgive him. Maybe he could give a hint of truth to this lie. He set his leg between hers as he tasted her body, and she ground her hips against him. She was either an incredible actress, determined not to flinch, or she truly wanted him.

He let one hand skim down her body to the edge of her chemise. He pulled it up, up, until his fingers slipped between her thighs.

She was not acting. She was silky wet. There was no space in his mind to encompass the wonder of her desire. He was lost, sliding his fingers through her curls until he found the spot that made her arch her back even more. He pinned her against the wall, pressing, tasting, touching, until she trembled, her breathing ragged. And then he sent her spinning over the edge.

She made a high, keening noise as she came.

A small sense of intelligence returned as she looked up at him. She was breathing heavily. Her skin glowed. Her chemise was rucked up to her waist. Her body pressed into his. He could feel her heart beat against his chest, feel her ribs expand with her every breath.

He was still dressed. His member was hard; his body screamed to sheathe himself deep inside her.

"William?"

No. He couldn't fool himself any longer. This was not some delicate virgin, submitting to his coarse lusts out of an excess of familial feeling. This was Lavinia. She was robust, and unbreakable. And for some unknown reason, she was not acting. She wanted him.

And he shouldn't take her. Not like this.

But when he pulled away, she followed. When he hesitated, she set her hands under his shirt. Her fingers slid up his abdomen, over his ribs. Any good intentions that might have entered his mind flared up in smoke, illuminating William's path to hell. He pulled off his shirt. The air was cold against his bare skin, but Lavinia was warm, and she was caressing him. Her hands slid to his waist. Her mouth found his again, and he could think of nothing but having her skin against his, her flesh pressed naked under his. He pulled his breeches off and pushed her onto the bed.

She landed and looked up at him. And then—time seemed so slow—she lifted off her chemise. Every fantasy he'd ever had compressed into this one moment. Lavinia Spencer was naked in his bed, lips parted, eyes shining. He spread her knees with his hands and leaned over her. He had a thousand fantasies, but only this one chance. He positioned his member against her hot, wet cleft.

He should not have been able to think of anything except the pleasure to come, but she looked into his eyes. Her look was so clear, so devoid of guile, that he stopped, arrested on the edge of consummation.

You don't have to do this.

He didn't know where the thought came from—perhaps some long-atrophied sense of right and wrong had exerted itself. The tip of his penis was wet with her juices. Her nipples had contracted into hard, rose-colored nubs and she lay beneath him, legs spread.

The next step would be so easy.

It was not just her innocence he would take. Lavinia's beauty was not a mere accident that arose from the fall of hair against shoulder, the curves of her breasts, the petals of her sex. No, even now, spread before him like an offering, she glowed with an inner light. Her appeal had as much to do with the innate trust she placed in those around her, in the way she smiled and greeted everyone as if they were worthy of her attention. If he took her, like this, he'd shatter her trust in the world. He would show her that men were fiends at heart, that there was no forgiveness in the world for sins committed by others.

You don't have to do this.

But men were fiends. And there was no forgiveness. He had never been granted any forgiveness.

He didn't have to do it, but he did it anyway. He slid into her in one firm thrust, and it was every bit as awful—and as good—as he'd imagined. It was wonderful, because she was sweet and hot and tight about him. It was wonderful, because she was his, now, in the most primal sense. But it was terrible, because he knew what he destroyed with that single thrust. Her hands came involuntarily between them, and he tensed and stopped.

"William." She touched his shoulders tentatively, as if he were the one who needed comfort. As if even his vile penetration could not shake her absurd trust in the world. And so he took her, thrusting into her. She clenched around him, the walls of her passage tight around his erection. She brought her hips up to his. And by God, that heat, that pulsing heat that wrapped around him, that cry she gave—it couldn't have been. She could not have come. But she had, and then he was pumping into her, loosing his seed into her womb, and crying out himself, hoarsely.

As his orgasm faded and his mind cleared of lust, he realized what a despicable man he was. He'd taken her like an animal. Oh, she'd let him—but what choice had he left her? He should have stopped. He should have let her go. Instead, he'd been so intent on himself that he hadn't cared what she wanted at all. He was as sorry a specimen as had ever been seen.

He pulled out of her and sat on the edge of the bed, his back to her.

The mattress sagged as she rearranged her weight. "William," she said.

He could not bring himself to turn around and see what he'd done. Would her eyes reflect the betrayal of trust?

"William," she said. "You must look at me. I have something to tell you."

He knew already what a despicable blackguard he was. He'd taken her virginity, and damn, he'd enjoyed it. But everything had a price, and the price of William's physical enjoyment would be this: her cold censure, and a speech that he hoped would cut him to ribbons. He deserved worse. And so he turned.

There was no judgment in her eyes—just a quiet, unfathomable serenity.

"When I told you my brother was not yet one-and-twenty," she said, "I did not intend to engage your sympathies. I was trying to point out that he is legally an infant. He is incapable of forming a contract. That promissory note is unenforceable."

William's mind went blank. Instead of thoughts, his head seemed to fill with water from the bottom of a lake—chilled liquid, dwelling where light could not filter.

"You had nothing to coerce me with," she continued. "You could not have done. No magistrate would have compelled my brother to pay the debt."

Her words skipped like stones over the surface of his thoughts. Hadn't he coerced her? He was sure he'd forced her into his bed. He deserved her condemnation. Damn it, he *wanted* it.

Instead, he was as empty as the wick of a candle that had just been extinguished. "Oh," he said. That one bare word didn't seem enough, so he added another. "Well." Other thoughts flitted through his mind, but they were also single syllables, and rather the sort that could not be uttered in front of a member of the gentler sex. Even if he had treated her in a most ungentle manner.

There was a vital difference between lust and love. It had been lust—desperate lust for her body—that had brought him to this point. Lust did not care about the loss of a woman's virtue. Lust did not care if a woman's feelings were wounded. Lust howled, and it wanted slaking. It didn't give a fig as to how the deed was accomplished. Lust was a beast, and one he'd nurtured well with a decade of resentment.

William thought of his four pounds ten a quarter—eighteen pounds per year of drudgery—and of the many years ahead of him while he garnered the recognition and the recommendations he would need so that he could one day become a man who earned…what, twenty-three pounds a year? He thought of the hole in Lavinia's glove, and her brother asking when she'd last had a new dress.

"Lavinia," he said carefully, "I don't deserve such a gift."

"Nobody gets gifts because he *deserves* them." She stood up and shook out her wrinkled chemise. "You get gifts because the giver wants to give them."

She wasn't arguing. She wasn't throwing herself at him. She wasn't weeping and carrying on. If she had done any of those things, he could have borne it. But she exuded a calm, cool competence that lay entirely outside William's understanding.

"I can't support a wife," he continued. "And even if I could, I'm not the man for you, Lavinia."

She reached for her dress. "I knew that the minute you tried to coerce me into your bed."

He shifted and fixed his gaze past her on the blighted tree outside his narrow window. "Then why did you agree to it? You had no need."

She had not trembled when he'd threatened her, when he'd made his horrible proposition. She had not shivered, not even when he'd claimed her body. But her hands betrayed the tiniest of tremors as she fastened her dress and reached for her cloak.

"No need? You said that everything worthwhile had a price. You were wrong. You are absolutely and without question the most completely misinformed man in all of creation. Everything really worth having," she said, "is *free.*"

"Free?"

"Given," she said, "without expectation of return." And she looked up at him, a fierce light in her eyes. "I wanted to show you."

That clear trust in her eyes was unbroken yet. He'd taken her virginity. How had she managed to keep her innocence?

"I have no notion what love is," he told her, almost in a panic. "None at all."

She picked up her cloak and shook it out. It flared about her shoulders and then fell, obscuring in thick wool the figure he had seen in such heartbreaking detail mere minutes before. "Well," she said. "Perhaps one day you'll figure it out."

And like that, she slipped past him. He listened, unmoving, as she stepped down the stairs and out of his life.

Chapter Three

IT WAS LATE AFTERNOON when Lavinia slowly climbed the stairs to the family rooms above the lending library. She ached all over, a vital, restless throb that twinged in every muscle.

"Lavinia?" Her father's weak call came from across the way. "Is that you?"

"Yes, Papa." She took off her cloak and hung it on a peg by the door. Half boots followed. "I went out on a...constitutional after service. I'll freshen up and join you shortly."

She ducked into her own room.

As far as the basics went, her small chamber was not so different from William's. The walls were whitewashed, the furniture plain and simple, and almost identical to his: washstand, bed, chair and a chest of drawers. Lavinia crossed to the other side of the room and poured water from a pitcher into the basin. As she washed, she examined her reflection in the mirror.

She knew what she was *supposed* to see. This was the face of a girl who'd been ruined. A woman of easy virtue.

The face that peeked back at her looked exactly the same as the one she'd seen in the mirror this morning. There was no giant proclamation writ across her forehead, denouncing her as unchaste. Her eyes did not glow a diabolical red. They weren't even demonically pink. And her body still felt as though it belonged to her—sore, yes, and tingling in ways that she'd never before experienced—but still hers. Perhaps more so.

He didn't love her.

Well. So? The reckless infatuation she'd felt hours before had been transmuted into something far more complex and…and cobwebby. She wasn't sure if the emotion that lodged deep in her gut was love. It felt more like longing. Maybe it had always been longing. In the year since he'd first started coming to their library, he'd looked at her. Until recently, however, he'd always looked away.

It had been an unpleasant surprise when he'd put his proposition to her so baldly—and so badly. But it hadn't taken her long to understand why he'd chosen to approach her in such a fundamentally uncouth manner. She'd realized with an unbearable certainty that he was deeply unhappy.

In generalities, her room was not so different from William's. But the specifics… There were nineteen years of memories stored in this room. A blue knit shawl, a gift from her father, draped over one side of her chest of drawers. A lopsided painting of daisies, a present James had given her two years ago, hung next to the mirror. A pine box on her nightstand contained all of Lavinia's jewelry—a gold chain and her late mother's wedding ring. These were not mere things, of course; they were memories, physical embodiments of the nineteen years that Lavinia had lived. They were proof that people loved her. Her brother had similar items in his room—a stone he'd picked up years ago on the beach in Brighton, the pearl pendant he'd inherited from his mother, to one day give his wife, and the penknife Lavinia had scrimped to buy him.

Where did William keep his memories? There had been nothing—not so much as a pressed flower—in his quarters. Not a single physical item indicated that he passed through life in contact with others. He must hold his memories entirely inside him.

It seemed a dreadfully lonesome place to keep them.

Things had emotional heft. Lavinia did not imagine a man avoided all mementos because he had been blessed with an inordinate number of good memories. That William had felt compelled to resort to blackmail, when she'd been so giddily inclined to him, said rather more about the light in which he saw himself than how he saw her. For all the harshness of his words, he'd touched her as if he worshipped her. He'd caressed her and held her and brought her to a pleasure that still had her limbs trembling. He might claim to have had no notion of love, but he'd not approached her as if her touches were credits on a balance sheet.

"Vinny?" James swung her door open without so much as a knock.

Luckily, the same absorption that led James to ignore Lavinia's privacy meant he did not notice her dress was overwrinkled. He did not look in her eyes and see the telltale glow that lit them.

"Vinny," he said again, "have you taken care of my note yet? Because I could—I mean, I *should* help."

And how could she answer? *She* hadn't taken care of his note. But James wouldn't have to worry about the matter ever again. As for William…

Lavinia pasted a false smile across her lips. "You have nothing to worry about," she said, "It's all taken care of. He's all taken care of."

Or he would be soon.

⌘ ⌘ ⌘

IT SEEMED INCONCEIVABLE TO WILLIAM that life should continue on as usual the morning after he'd damned himself. The night passed nonetheless. The London streets a few blocks over awoke and rumbled as a hundred sellers prepared for market. Not only did the clock continue on schedule, but—as if fate itself were laughing up its sleeve at him—they marched inexorably on to Monday morning.

Monday. After he'd betrayed all finer points of civilization, nothing so trivial as a Monday morning should have been allowed to exist. And yet Monday persisted.

When William stepped on the streets, he shrank into the shoulders of his coat and pulled his hat over his eyes. But as he walked down Peter Street, nobody raised the hue and cry. No cries of "Stop! Despoiler of women!" followed his steps. Yesterday he'd snared an innocent woman in his bed by the foulest of means. Today nobody even gave him a second glance.

Up until the moment when William arrived at the gray Portland stone building where he worked, just opposite Chancery Lane, the day seemed a Monday much like every other Monday that had come before: gray, dreary and unfortunately necessary. But as soon as William opened the door to the office, he knew that this was not going to be an ordinary Monday.

It was going to be worse. Everyone, from Mr. Dunning, the manager, to Jimmy, the courier boy, sat stiffly. There were no jokes, no exchanged conversations. David Holder, one of William's fellow clerks, inclined his head ever so slightly to the left.

There stood his employer. The elderly Marquess of Blakely was solid and ever so slightly stooped with age. If one were boasting in a tavern, the man might have seemed the most respectable master, the sort that any employee would feel proud to serve. When William had first arrived, he'd spun a fantasy in which his keen mind and meticulous work made him indispensable to the marquess. In his dreamworld, he'd been granted promotions, advances in wages. He'd won the respect of everyone around him.

That dream had been exceedingly short in duration. It had lasted a week from the day he was hired—until he'd met the man.

The old marquess was a tyrant. In his mind, he didn't employ servants; he grudgingly shelled out money for minions. The marquess didn't merely demand the obeisance and courtesy due his station; he required groveling. And, every so often, instead of raising a man up for skill and dedication, he chose an employee and delved into his work until he found an error—and no worker, however conscientious, was ever perfect—and then let the man loose. William and his fellow servants went to work every day swallowing fear for breakfast.

Fear did not sit well on a belly and heart as empty as William's was today. He stood frozen in the old marquess's gray-browed sights.

"Ah." Old as he was, the marquess's gaze did not waver, not in the slightest. It was William who dropped his eyes, of course, bobbing his head in hated obeisance. He fumbled hastily with his hat, pulling it from his head. For a long while the elderly lord simply stared at him. William wasn't sure if he should offer the insult of turning his back so he could hang up his hat, or if he must stand icebound in place, headgear uncomfortably clutched in his hands.

The marquess turned his head, looking at William side on. With that shock of graying hair, the pose reminded William of some dirty-white bird of prey. The image wouldn't have bothered him quite so much if William hadn't felt like so much worm to the other man's raptor.

His lordship glanced away, and William gulped air in relief. But instead of moving his attention to another man, the marquess simply pulled a watch from his pocket.

"Whoever you are," he announced, "you're a minute late to your seat."

I wouldn't have been had you not glowered at me. But William held his tongue. He couldn't afford to lose his position. "I apologize, my lord. It won't happen again."

"No, it won't." The marquess gave the words a rather more sinister complexion. "Blight, is it?"

"Actually, it's White, my lord. William White."

He should not have offered correction. Lord Blakely's eyes narrowed.

"Ah, yes. Bill Blight."

He spoke as if William had not worked for him these three years. As if instead of names, his employees were possessed of empty pages, and the marquess could fill those bleak tablets with any syllables he found convenient.

"Come into the back office," the marquess said calmly. "And do bring the books you've worked on for the last two years."

An invitation to the back office was as good as a death sentence. It felt like an eternity that William stood, fixed in space. But what good would it to do to scream or shout? If he went quietly, Mr. Dunning might help him find another position when he was sacked.

How ironic, that he'd divested himself so unthinkingly of those ten pounds, when he might find them of such immediate use. No—not ironic. It was the opposite of ironic.

Perhaps it was appropriate that he'd been singled out. He wasn't fit for polite society, after all. Not after what he'd done to Lavinia. How could he ever make it up to her? Maybe this, finally, was the censure he'd been expecting all morning. He'd accept whatever came his way as his just due.

Once inside the back office, the marquess picked one of the books at random. He thumbed through it slowly, his fat fingers pausing every so often, before moving onward. William stared past him. The room's furnishings could well have been as old as the marquess. The wallpaper had long gone brown, and dry curls of paper at the edge of the baseboard were working their way off the wall.

Finally the lord lifted his head. "You seem to do good work," the old Lord Blakely said. Said by anyone else, it would be a compliment. But William's employer twisted the sentence in his mouth, giving a slight emphasis to the word *seem*. By the ugly glint in his eye, William knew he was adding his own caveat: *I am not fooled by your apparent competence.*

"Tell me," the marquess continued. "On September 16, 1821, you entered three transactions related to the home-farm in Kent. I'd like a few specifics."

Fifteen months ago. The man focused on transactions made fifteen bloody months ago? How could William possibly recall the details of a transaction more than a year in age? One did not keep books so that one could browbeat the person who entered a transaction.

One didn't unless one happened to be the Marquess of Blakely.

"It is the first transaction, for two pounds six, that I—"

The door opened quietly behind them, interrupting his speech.

The old marquess looked up. His fists clenched on the account book, and his eyes widened. He drew himself up, undoubtedly to castigate the fool who had the temerity to interrupt this ritual sacrifice. William drew his breath in, thinking he'd won a reprieve. If he had, the intruder would undoubtedly take on William's punishment. Whoever it was walked forward, steady, heavy footsteps crossing the room. A mixture of shame and relief flooded William. Perhaps he might keep his position—but it was a sorry man who hoped his carcass would be saved because a shark choked on another fish first. It was an even sorrier man who hoped so, knowing that of all the fellows in the office, he was most deserving of punishment.

But instead of one of William's fellow clerks or the estate manager, the young man who came abreast of William's chair was the one person the old marquess could not sack.

It was his eldest grandson. William had seen the man only once, and at a distance. But he'd been accounting for the details of the man's funds for three years. Gareth Carhart. Viscount Wyndleton, for now. The man was a few years younger than William. He had attended Harrow, then Cambridge. He had a substantial fortune, received a comfortable allowance from his grandfather, and he would inherit the marquessate. William almost felt as if he knew the fellow. He was certain he held the young, privileged lord in dislike.

The young viscount might have had a hundred servants available to do his bidding. But incongruously, the man was carrying his own valise. He set this luggage on the ground and placed his hands gently on his grandfather's desk.

No thumping, no shouting, no untoward drama of any sort. Had William not been a mere foot away, he would not even have detected the rigid tension in the muscles on the backs of his hands.

"Thank you very much." The viscount's words were quiet—not unemotional, William realized, but so suffused with emotion that only that flat, invariant tone could contain his disdain. "I appreciate your telling the carriage drivers not to take me to Hampshire. I applaud your decision to bribe—how many was it? It must have been every owner of a private conveyance in London, so that they would not take me, either. But it took real genius on your part to outright purchase the Hampshire coach lines in their entirety, five days before Christmas."

"Well." The old Lord Blakely preened and examined his nails. Of course, the man did not find anything so uncouth as dirt near his fingers, but he nonetheless brushed away an imagined speck. "How lovely of you to admit my intelligence. Now do you believe that I was serious when I told you that if you did not give up your foolish scientific pursuits, you would not see that woman?"

William might have drowned in the sea of their exchanged sarcasm. Neither man seemed to care that he was in the room. He was invisible—a servant, a hired man. He might have been etched on the curling wallpaper, for all the attention that they paid him.

The young viscount lifted his chin. "That woman," he said carefully, "is my *mother.*"

William felt a twinge of satisfaction. He ought not to have reveled in the other man's pain, but it was delicious to know that even money could not buy freedom.

"I'm leaving," Lord Wyndleton continued.

"No, you are not. What you are doing is throwing a tantrum, like a child demanding a boiled sweet. It is long past time that you gave up that natural philosophy nonsense and learned to manage an estate like a lord."

"I can read a damned account book."

"Yes, but can you manage seventeen separate properties? Can you keep a host of useless and unmotivated servitors bent to their tasks?"

The young viscount's gaze cut briefly toward William. William felt himself analyzed, cataloged—

and then, just as swiftly, dismissed, an obstacle as irrelevant and underwhelming as a dead black beetle lying in the middle of a thoroughfare.

"How difficult can it be?"

"Bill Blight, why don't you explain to my grandson what I had planned for you?"

"You were, I believe, going to look through my work until you found an error. My lord." *And then you were going to turn me off.*

"Blight, tell him what I really intended."

William pressed his lips together. "You were going to sack me to induce terror in your staff."

That sort of sentence—bald and unforgiving—ought to have gotten him tossed out on his ear.

Instead, the marquess smiled. "Precisely so. Wyndleton, how do you suppose I managed to thwart your ill-fated flight this morning? I assure you, I did not need to bribe every driver in London. I keep my staff in line—and that means they do as I say, what I say, no matter the cost."

The young viscount's nostrils flared.

"You think you can be a marquess? Like that?" The marquess snapped his fingers. "Get your valise. Spend these two days with me—do as I say—and you'll start to learn how it's done. Someday you might even get to thwart me. Or you would, if you had the money to do it."

Still Lord Wyndleton did not move. He stood next to William, his arms rigid, his fingers curving into the desk like claws.

"Come along," the marquess said. "I shouldn't have to spoon-feed you these lessons. If you'll listen to me, I'll have the carriage take you over late Christmas Eve." The old man stood up and walked to the door. He didn't look back.

After all, William thought bitterly, what else could mere mortals do but jump to perform his bidding? The thought almost put him in charity with the man standing nearby. The viscount slowly straightened.

"What I don't understand," William said quietly, "is why you don't buy your own carriage."

Lord Wyndleton turned to him. This close, William could see the golden brown of his eyes—predator's eyes, or at least, a predator in training. Like any wolf cub caught in a trap, he snapped in anger at anything that came near.

"He's holding the purse strings, you idiot." He straightened and wiped his hands on his sleeves. "My grandfather is sacking you, yes?"

"He'll get around to it."

Gareth Carhart, Viscount Wyndleton, picked up the valise. He nodded sharply. "Excellent," he said, and then he walked out of the room.

⌘ ⌘ ⌘

THE END OF THE DAY ARRIVED, but Lord Blakely and his grandson still had not returned. This meant that William had still not been sacked.

Winter struck directly through William's coat as he left his place of employment. Yes, he'd had a reprieve—albeit a temporary one. He knew the marquess's tactics. Once he got a man in his sights, he did not let up. Today William survived. Tomorrow… It was going to be another damned cold night, one in a string of damned cold nights stretching from this moment until death.

"Mr. White."

William turned. There, in virulent yellow waistcoat, burgeoning over an ample belly, his locks pomaded to glossy slickness, stood Mr. Sherrod's solicitor. The corner of William's lip turned up in an involuntary snarl.

"Do you have another taunt to deliver on your late employer's behalf?" William pulled his coat around him and started walking away, brushing past the unctuous fellow. "As it is, I must be on my way."

The solicitor's hand shot out and grabbed his wrist. "Nonsense, Mr. White. I've come to a realization. A *profitable* realization. I wanted to…to share it with you."

William stared at the chubby fingers on his cuff, and then carefully picked them off his sleeve, one by one. The digits felt greasy even through his gloves.

"Adam Sherrod," the man said, "left the bulk of his fortune in his final testament to the serious little stick of a woman who served as his wife. Given the informal agreement he made with your father, you might contest the disposition of his estate. I had, in point of fact, hoped that you would. You accepted your fate with surprising grace the other day."

"Is there any chance of overturning the testament? I assume the document was valid and witnessed. And it was only an informal agreement between the two men, after all. I've heard that excuse often enough."

"Hmm." The man looked away and rubbed his lips. "To speak with perfect plainness, you could claim he was not in his right mind. You see, before he married, he actually had intended to keep his word. He'd left you half his fortune, five thousand pounds. It would be easy to argue that he did not see sense. After all, he did marry *her*. Overturn his latest version of the will, and you stand to win a great deal."

In William's experience, any time someone claimed to speak perfectly plainly, his words were rarely plain and never perfect. First, Adam Sherrod had been merely despicable, and not mad. Even setting aside this tiny detail of reality, the solicitor's suggestion felt as oily as his hair. It took William a moment to pinpoint why he was uneasy.

"You're his solicitor," he accused. "You're the trustee of the estate, are you not? This advice of yours cannot be in the estate's interest. Why are you giving it?"

The man licked his lips. "Mr. White. Must you ask? I don't like to see an upstanding young man deprived of what ought rightfully to be his. It doesn't sit well with my conscience."

The solicitor bounced on his toes and lifted his chin, unburdened by anything so heavy as a sense of right and wrong. William kept silent, staring at the man. The man rubbed the back of his neck uneasily. He shifted from foot to foot.

That dance of guilt was all too familiar to William. He'd felt that itch. The knowledge that he'd made an irretrievable error had nestled deep in his stomach all day. He'd *known* what he'd done to Lavinia had been wrong as he was doing it. He'd done it anyway.

"At what point in your legal apprenticeship did you acquire a conscience, then? And when did you first betray it?"

"Well. It's not so much a betrayal as…as a renegotiation, if you will. If you must know the truth, if you could tie up the estate in Chancery, the fees to the trustee from administration of her estate would be substantial. It's a profitable plan for us both. I'll protest, naturally, for form's sake. And you—you'll be able to strike an open blow at the man who had you put out on the streets when you were fourteen. You could have him declared mad, and destroy his reputation."

Greasy though the man was, he knew how to tempt William. There would be a delightful symmetry in ruining Mr. Sherrod's legacy just as William's father's had been ruined.

"And then what?" William demanded.

"Well, after a short, insignificant delay in the courts of Chancery—really nothing to speak of—you'll get his five thousand pounds."

"A short, insignificant delay," William said drily. "Naturally. Chancery being known for its alacrity. And you must mean, five thousand pounds minus the tiny fees for estate administration that would accrue over that infinitesimal delay."

The solicitor bowed. "Precisely so."

It would hardly be so smooth. The process might take years. Still, the money called out to him. Five thousand pounds. Five thousand pounds in the safe four-percent funds translated into a good two hundred a year.

As if sensing William's temptation, the solicitor continued. "Think on the money. You could buy your own home. You would not need to labor like a common man. You could buy yourself a new coat."

The solicitor reached out and flicked William's sleeve, where the fabric had become shiny with age. William recoiled.

"Mr. White, you would need never feel cold again."

The man misunderstood the nature of temptation. It wasn't himself he clothed in new finery. Instead, his breath caught, thinking what he could give Lavinia. She could have any dress she wanted. Every last penny she deserved. He could fashion himself into a gentleman. He could become a man she would respect, instead of one she gifted with her virginity out of pity.

He need never feel cold again.

But then, there was a catch. There was always a catch, and this one stuck in his skin like some barbed thing. He'd have to enter into a collusion with this unnatural creature. He would have to lie to the court. He'd have to cheat Adam Sherrod's widow—his *innocent* widow—and dispossess her of funds that she deserved.

What did a little thing like his honor signify? He'd toss his own grandmother to hellhounds if it meant he could have Lavinia.

He'd won a reprieve from the marquess. Now he'd gotten this offer. A little oil, a little grease. What was a little extra dishonor, atop the mountain he'd already constructed for himself?

The solicitor jogged William's shoulder. "Don't take too long. It took me weeks to track you down. The time for filing an appeal is disappearing. Stop by my office tomorrow morning to go over the details."

William opened his mouth to say he'd do it. The words filled his mouth, bitter as rancid lard, but they would not come out. *I'll do it,* he thought. *I'll do it.*

He conjured up the thought of Lavinia—but he could not imagine how she would forgive him, promise of money or no. And with the money…if he agreed to this scheme, he'd not be able to wash the stench of this bug of a solicitor from his skin. How could he beg for her absolution if he could not even face himself?

How could he have her at all, if he did not accept this desperate possibility?

What he finally said was, "Tomorrow. I'll decide tomorrow."

⌘   ⌘   ⌘

THE LIBRARY BUSTLED WITH CUSTOMERS that Monday evening—six of them, to be precise—and they kept Lavinia very busy indeed, as none were willing to browse on his own. She was reaching up, up for the newest set of Byron's poetry when she heard the shop door open behind her.

A blast of cold air greeted this newest arrival. Yet it was not the temperature that had Lavinia's skin breaking out in gooseflesh. Without looking, she knew it was *him*. She froze, hand above her head. Her heart raced. But she could not react, not in this room, not with all these people here. And so she retrieved the leather-bound volume and handed it to Mr. Adrian Bellows before she allowed herself to turn.

Mr. William Q. White was as tall and taciturn as ever. This time, though, *he* caught her glance and ducked his head, coloring.

Oh, how the tables had turned. Two days ago she'd been the one to blush and turn away. Two days ago *she* had wondered, in her own giddy and foolish way, what he thought of her.

But then yesterday they'd come together, skin against skin. He'd had her; she'd had him.

Today the question on her mind was: What did *she* think of *him*?

It was not a query with an easy answer. He dawdled until the others trickled out, one by one. Even then he did not approach her. Instead, he studied a shelf of Greco-Roman histories so intently, she wondered if their spines contained the secrets of the universe. When she walked toward him, he turned his back to her. He bent, ever so slightly, as if he carried a great weight in his jacket.

Lavinia supposed he did.

"I am sorry," he said, still faced away from her. "I ought not to have come. If my presence distresses you, say so and I shall leave at once."

"I am not easily distressed." She kept her voice calm and even.

He turned toward her and looked in her face, as if to ascertain for himself whether she was telling the truth. "Are you well?" His voice was low, lilting in that accent that he had. "I could not sleep, thinking of what I had done to you."

She had not slept, either, reliving what he had done, touching herself where he had touched. But the expression on his face suggested that his evening had not been spent nearly so pleasurably.

"I am very well," she said. And then, because he looked away, his eyes tightening in obvious distress, she added, "Thank you for asking."

Politeness didn't seem enough after what had passed between them, but she was unsure of the etiquette for this occasion.

"Miss Spencer, I know I can never hope for forgiveness. I dishonored you—"

"Strange," Lavinia interjected, "that I do not feel dishonored."

He frowned as if puzzled, and then started again. "I ruined you—"

"Ruined me for what? I am still capable of working in this shop, as you see. I do not believe I shall turn toward prostitution as a result of one afternoon's pleasure. And as for marriage—William, do you truly think that any man worth having would put me aside for one indiscretion?"

"Put you aside?" His gaze skittered down her breasts to her waist, and then traveled slowly up. "No. He would take you any way he could have you."

She was not one bit sorry that she'd given herself to this man, however foolish and impulsive the gift had been.

"As I see it," Lavinia said carefully, "you are feeling guilty because you attempted to coerce me into your bed. Then, believing I was forced, you took me anyway."

He flinched, looking away again. "Yes. And for that, I ought to be—"

"I was not forced, and so you did not dishonor me."

"But—"

"But," Lavinia said, holding up one finger, "you believed I was, and thus you dishonored yourself."

His expression froze. His eyes shut and he put his hand over his face. A shaky breath whispered through his fingers. "Ah." It was not a sound of understanding or agreement, but one of despair. "You are very astute."

There was nothing to say beyond that, but he looked so unbearably alone that she reached out and placed her hand atop his.

He shut his eyes. "Don't." His hand bunched into a fist underneath hers, but he did not pull away. Apparently, "don't" was William Q. White for "keep touching me." Lavinia pressed her hand against the heat of his knuckles.

"Tell me," he said presently, "the other evening when you told the young Mr. Spencer that you had a plan, why did you not tell him immediately he could not be held accountable?"

It took Lavinia a few seconds to remember what he was talking about—the moment when James had first presented her with his idiocy.

"Why would I have told him? I would have taken care of it. He didn't need to know any details. It was simply a matter of deciding upon an approach."

"You would have done everything yourself? Without assistance?"

Since her mother had died this year past, Lavinia had assisted everyone else. She had assisted in the library, until her father's illness destroyed all pretense that she was a mere assistant. She had assisted with housekeeping; she had assisted her younger brother in his lessons, and bailed him out of the sort of scrapes that younger brothers occasionally got into. She had never begrudged them the time she spent; she did it because she loved her family.

She wasn't sure she knew how to let someone help her instead.

She tightened her hand about his, letting his warmth seep into her. "Of course I'd have done it alone."

"Tell me." His voice dropped even lower, and she leaned in to listen. "If I had offered that evening—would you have let me assist you?"

She looked up into his eyes. He watched her with that expression in his eyes—desire, she realized, and dark despair that ran so deeply, it was almost outside detection. He wasn't asking out of an idle desire to know.

"But you didn't. You didn't offer."

He shut his eyes.

And then the door burst open, and William snatched his fingers from hers. She pulled her hands away and tucked them behind her back with alacrity and jumped away.

James darted through the entry, his face a picture of excitement. But even he was sufficiently observant to see she'd sprung from William like a guilty child. It was easy to think of him as her younger brother, as a child. But when he looked from Lavinia to William, his lips thinning, she realized he was not as young as he'd once been.

"We're closed," he said, in a chilly tone of voice. "And you—whoever you are—you're leaving."

Before Lavinia could protest, William had pulled away and was walking out the door.

James looked her over, his gaze resting first on her flushed cheeks and then on the telltale way she put her hands behind her back. Then he cast a glance of pure scorn at William's back. "I'm leaving, too," he announced, and he followed William out the door, into the cold.

Chapter Four

LAVINIA'S BROTHER, WILLIAM THOUGHT WRYLY, was a thin spike of a boy. Attach a sufficient quantity of straw to his head, and he'd have made a passable broom. In polite society, he might have served as a chaperone, a place-holder designed to do little more than observe. But James Spencer, this pale wraith of a child, apparently believed he could *protect* his sister from someone who threatened her virtue. He had been alarmingly misled. Standing outside Spencer's on the freezing pavement, James folded his arms—a posture that only emphasized the sharp skin-and-bone of his shoulders.

There was a saying, William supposed, about guarding the cows after the wolves had already come a-ravening. The adage seemed rather inappropriate as cows could only be eaten once. He'd promised himself he'd not importune her again, but one touch of her hand and he'd been ready to go a-ravening all over again.

James tapped his toe, frowning. "Did you kiss her?"

Oh, the barren and virtuous imagination of callow youth.

"Yes," William said. It was easier than resorting to explanation.

James peered dubiously at William, as if trying to ascertain whether there truly was a patch on his coat. "And what are your prospects?"

"Too dismal to take a wife. Even if I chose to do so, which—at present—I do not."

Lavinia's brother gasped. If the boy thought kissing a woman without wanting to marry her constituted open devilry, God forbid he ever learn what had really transpired.

"If you're not going to marry her," he said, shocked, "then why'd you kiss her?"

William had long suspected it, but now he was certain. Lavinia's younger brother was an idiot.

"Mr. Spencer." William spoke slowly, searching for small words that were nonetheless sharp enough to penetrate her brother's dim cogitation. "Kissing is a pleasant activity. It is considerably more pleasant when the woman one is kissing is more than passably pretty. Your sister happens to be the loveliest lady in all of London. Why do you suppose I kissed her?"

"My sister?"

"You needn't pull such a face. It's not something to admit in polite company, but we're both men here." At least, James would be one day. "You know it's the truth."

"No," James said incredulously, screwing up his eyes. "You want to kiss my *sister*? I never thought—"

"Well, you'd better start thinking about it, you little fool. *Everyone* wants to kiss your sister. And what are you doing to protect her? Nothing."

"I'm protecting her now!"

"You leave her in that shop with nobody to call for if she needs help except your father, who is too ill to respond. You send her out to capture your vowels from known ruffians who live near docks where sailors cavort. Don't tell me you protect your sister. How many times have I found her alone in the library? Do you have any idea what I could have done to her?"

He was angry, William realized. Furious that he'd been allowed to take from her the most precious thing she could give, and angrier still that nobody—least of all Lavinia—was willing to castigate him for it.

"I could have taken a great deal more than a kiss," he said. "Easily."

James's face paled. "You wouldn't. You couldn't."

He had. He *would*. He wanted to do it again.

It felt good to admit what a blackguard he was, even if he was hiding his confession behind safely conditional statements. "Lock the door and anything becomes possible," William said. "I could have had—"

James punched him in the stomach. For a skinny fellow, he struck hard. The blow knocked the wind out of William's lungs and he doubled over. That punch was the first real punishment he'd suffered since he'd had Lavinia. Thank God. He deserved worse.

When he regained his breath and his balance, he looked up. "Don't tell me you protect your sister. You put everything on her—the burden of caring for your entire family—and give her nothing in exchange. I've seen her. I know what you do."

James stood over him. "If you're such a blackguard, why are you telling me this?"

"Because I'll go to the devil before Lavinia kisses a scoundrel worse than me."

James stopped and cocked his head. In that instant William saw in the boy's posture something of Lavinia—a chance similarity, perhaps, in the way his eyes seemed to penetrate through William's skin. William felt suddenly translucent, as if all of his foolish wants, his wistful longing for Lavinia, were laid out in neat rows for this boy's examination. He didn't want to see those feelings himself. He surely didn't want this child sitting in judgment over affections that could never be.

William shook his head. "No."

Her brother had not said a word, but still William felt he must deny what had gone unspoken. "Don't look at me like that. I can't care for her, you idiot, so you'd better start."

James could not have accrued any substance to his frame in these few minutes. Still, when he lifted his chin, he looked taller. "Don't worry," he said quietly. "I will."

⌘　⌘　⌘

LAVINIA HEARD HER BROTHER'S FOOTSTEPS fall heavily on the stairs that led to their living quarters. James had seen her embracing a strange man. Half an hour ago he'd followed William outside. Now he was coming back, and she didn't have answers for any of the questions he might put to her. She didn't want to defend her virtue tonight. Instead she stared at the account books in front of her. Industriousness would ward off any hard questions.

She forced herself to concentrate on the numbers in front of her. *Five plus six plus thirteen made four-and-twenty....*

The door squeaked behind James, and then closed.

Four-and-twenty plus twelve plus seventeen was fifty-three.

He crossed the room and stood behind her. She could hear the quiet rush of a resigned exhalation. Still, Lavinia pretended she couldn't hear him. Yes, that was it. She was so engrossed in the books that she didn't even notice he was breathing down her neck.

Fifty-three and fifteen made sixty-eight.

"Vinny," James said quietly. "I don't think you should always be the one to slave away over these books. Isn't it about time I began to take over?"

No accusations. It would have been easier if she'd been able to lie to him. Lavinia carefully laid her pen down and turned to her brother. His eyes were large, not with accusation, but with the weight of responsibility. She'd wanted to save him from that.

"Oh, James." Lavinia arranged the lapels of his damp coat into some semblance of order. "That's very sweet of you."

"I'm not being sweet. It's necessary. I need to be able to manage without you."

Why? I can do it better.

She caught the words before they came out of her mouth. How many times had James offered to help, in his awkward way? How many times had she refused him? She couldn't even count.

"After all," he continued, his voice slow, "you might marry."

"I'm not getting married." Her denial came too fast; her light tone sounded too forced. He'd *seen* her with William. And even though he hadn't actually caught them kissing, they'd been clasping hands in easy intimacy. How was she supposed to explain to her younger brother she had engaged in such conduct with a man she was not marrying? Best to talk of something else.

But before she could offer up even the most ham-handed change of subject, James let out a slow breath. "Still. Should I not help?"

What had William said about them? Oh God. Had he told James the embarrassing details? Lavinia's hand shook, ever so slightly, where it rested on her brother's coat. "You're right. Maybe I can assign you some task—something small."

He frowned and folded his arms. "I should have thought you would be happy to step down."

Step down? Step down! That would ruin *everything*. Her brother had no notion how to argue with creditors for a favorable repayment schedule; he'd not learned how to account precisely for the location of every volume in the library. If she left the shop to him, he'd lose a ha'penny here, a ha'penny there, until the flow of cash dried up. The library would falter and then fail. Everything she'd worked for would fall to pieces.

James didn't seem aware he'd just proposed complete disaster. He continued on, as if he were a reasonable person. "I think I should be able to handle the work very well. I *am* almost sixteen years of age."

"James." In her ears, her voice sounded flat and emotionless. "I can't step down. There are too many things to remember."

"So you can tell me what to do at first."

"I can't tell you everything! Would you think to save pennies each day, so we might have a Christmas celebration? Would you think to bargain with the apothecary, giving him priority on the new volumes in exchange for a discount on medicines?"

She could see his fine plans crumbling, his desire to do more faltering. He drew his brows down. "Would it be so awful, then, if I made a mistake or two? I just want to do my part."

Lavinia shut the account book in front of her. "If it weren't for your mistakes," she said, her voice shaking, "we'd be having a real celebration on

Christmas, just like Mother gave us. It would be as if she were not gone. Now we're having nothing. Why do you suppose I'm staring at the accounts, if not to conjure up the coins you lost?"

His face flushed with embarrassment and anger. "I said I was sorry already. What more do you want from me? You're not my mother. Stop acting as if you are."

"That's not fair. I'm just trying to make you happy." She wasn't sure when her voice had started to rise, when she had begun to clench her hands.

Her brother shook his head. "You're doing a bang-up job of that, then. So far, all you've managed to do is make me miserable." He stomped away. He couldn't get far; the flat was simply too small. He paused on the edge of his chamber, and then turned. "I despise you," he said. A second later the door to his chamber slammed. The walls rattled.

Lavinia curled her arms around herself. He didn't hate her. He wasn't miserable. He was just…momentarily upset?

"One day," she said softly, "you will understand how idyllic your childhood has been. You have nothing to worry about. That's what I've saved you from."

She clenched her hands around the account book, the leather binding biting into her palms. Then she opened the book carefully and found the spot where she'd left off adding columns.

Fifty-three and fifteen made sixty-six….

⌘ ⌘ ⌘

EVERY TIME LAVINIA AWOKE THAT NIGHT, tossing and turning in her narrow bed, she remembered her words to William. *You thought you had forced me, and thus you dishonored yourself.* She could call to mind the precise curl of his mouth as he'd realized what he'd done, the exact shape of his hands as he grasped the dimensions of his dishonor.

She had wanted to lessen his hurt, but she'd made it worse.

All you have managed to do is make me miserable. Not William's words, but they seemed to apply all the same.

No, no, no. Lavinia stood and walked to her window. Thick, choking fog filled her vision. It was past midnight, and thus it was now Christmas Eve. But it was not yet near morning. The night fog was so thick it would swallow an entire troupe of players juggling torches. It could easily hide one nineteen-year-old woman who didn't want to be seen. She *would* make William feel better. She had to.

Silently she opened her bedroom door. She crept out into the main room and removed her cloak from its peg. She found her boots with her toe, and then bent to pick them up. Slowly she crept down the not-quite-creaking stairs, and across the lending library. And then she was outside, the fog enshrouding her in its cold embrace.

Lavinia lifted her chin, put on her boots and walked. In the few nights before Christmas, a musicians' company sent men on the streets to play through the darkness of night. There were no players anywhere near her house, of course, but in these quiet hours before dawn, the haunting sound of twin recorders came to her in tiny snatches. The sound wafted through the fog like fairy music. She'd catch a bar, but before the melody resolved itself into a recognizable tune, it slipped away, melting into the fog like the shadow of a Christmas that had not yet come.

As she walked through the engulfing mist, those enchanted notes grew fainter and fainter. By the time she reached Norwich Court, they had disappeared altogether.

When she arrived at his home, she realized she had no key to unlock his door. Surely, his chamber was too distant for him to hear her knock.

A little thing like impossibility had never stopped Lavinia.

She was systematically testing the windows when the creak of a door opening sounded behind her.

"Lavinia?" His voice.

She turned, her stomach churning in anticipation at the sound of her name on his lips. He stood, four feet away from her, his form barely visible through the fog. She jumped down from her uncomfortable perch on the windowsill, and would have run into his arms—but he'd crossed them in a most forbidding manner. Instead, she walked slowly toward him, her heart pounding.

"You must be freezing." His words reeked of disapproval. "Thank God I couldn't sleep again.

Thank God you didn't meet anyone on your way over. If you were my—"

She had come close enough that she saw the scowl flit over his face at that. He shut his mouth and turned away, walking into the house.

She followed. "If I were your *wife*," she threw at his retreating back, "I wouldn't need to risk all this fog just to see you on a morning."

He didn't respond. But he left the door open, and she went after him. This time, he had not climbed the stairs to his bedchamber. He was headed down a narrow cramped hall into the back of the house. Lavinia sighed and closed the door behind her.

She was not his wife. She was not even anything to him so clean and uncomplicated as his sweetheart. She was the woman who'd made his life miserable. Still, she followed him down the hall. The narrow passage gave way to a tiny kitchen in the back of the house. Without looking at her, he pulled a chair out from under a narrow, wooden table and placed it directly by the hearth. She sat; he stoked the fire and then placed a kettle on the grate.

For a long while he only stared into the orange ribbons that arched away from the flames. The dancing light painted his profile in glimmering yellow. His lips pressed together. His eyes were hooded. Then he shook his head and stabbed the coals with a poker. Bright sparks flew.

"If you were my wife," he finally said, "this moment would be a luxury—enough coal of a morning to heat the room."

He shook his head, set the poker down and turned away. William moved about the tiny room with the efficiency of a man used to dealing for himself. He set out a pot and cups, and then turned back to her. "If you were my wife, you'd take your bread without butter. You would mend your gloves three, four, five times over, until the material became more darn than fabric. And when the babes came, we'd have to remove from even these tiny and insupportable quarters into a part of London that is even less safe than this address. We'd have no other way to support a family."

"When the babes came?" Those words sent a happy thrill through her.

He turned to contemplate the fire again. "I am not such a fool as to imagine they wouldn't. Lavinia, if you were my wife, the babes would come. And come. And come. I couldn't keep my hands off you. I pray one is not already on the way."

It was not her fog-dampened cloak that left her chilled. He spoke of putting his hands on her as if she were one more bitter sip from a cup that was already starkly devoid of happiness.

"It would be worth it," she said quietly. "The gloves. The bread. It would be worth it to me for the touch of your hands alone."

"Is that why you came here this morning?" He spoke in tones equally low to hers. "Did you come here so that I would touch you?"

Yes. Or she'd come to touch him—to see if she could salvage the moment when he'd thought himself dishonored. He'd said once he had no notion of love. She'd wanted to show him.

"Did you come thinking I would kiss your lips? That I would undo the ties of your cloak and let my hands slide down your skin?"

Her body heard, and it answered. The heat of the fire flickered against her neck; she imagined its warm touch was his hands. She imagined his hands tracing down her cheek; his hands cupping the curve of her bodice and warming her breasts; his hands coaxing her nipples into hard points. She ached in tune with his every word. Her breath grew fast.

He knelt on the floor in front of her, one knee on the ground. With that frozen, almost supercilious expression on his face, his posture seemed a gross parody of a proposal of marriage.

"In the year since I first saw you," he said, "I have imagined your giving yourself to me a thousand times. If these were my wildest dreams, I'd have you now. On that chair. I would spread your legs and nibble my way from your thigh to your sex. I'd slip inside you. And when I'd had my way with you, I would thank the Lord for the bruises on my knees."

As he spoke, her legs parted. Her sex tingled. His breath quickened to match hers. *Do it. Yes, do it.*

He reached out one hand and laid it on her knee. It was the first time he'd touched her all morning, and her whole body thrilled in wicked recognition of his. She leaned forward. For one eternal second, she could taste his breath, hot and masculine, on the tip of her tongue. She stretched to meet him. But before her lips found his, he stood.

"Lavinia." His words sounded like a reproach. "I can't have you in dishonor. I can't have you in poverty. And so I will not be marrying you."

She stared up into his eyes. Those dark mahogany orbs seemed so far away, so implacable. She *had* to fix this. But before she could speak, a hissing, sputtering noise intruded from her left, and he turned away from her.

It was the kettle, boiling with inappropriate merriment over the fire. He found a cloth. For a few minutes, he busied himself with the kettle and teapot, his back to her.

When he finally turned back, he held a cup in his hands.

"Here," he said. "The very nectar of poverty. Five washings of the leaves. I believe the liquid still has some flavor." He handed it to her. "There's no sugar. There's never any sugar."

She took the cup. He pulled his hand away quickly, before she could clasp it against the clay. In her hands, the warm mug radiated heat. Tiny black dots, the dust of broken tea leaves, swirled in the beverage.

"You don't speak like a poor man." She darted a gaze up at him. "You don't *read* like a poor man, either. Malthus. Smith. Craig. *The Annals of Agriculture.*"

He turned away from her to pour his own cup of tea. He did not drink it. "When I was fourteen, my father, a tradesman who aspired to be more, engaged in some rather risky speculation. A friend of his had lured him in. He promised to see me through my schooling, and to settle some significant amount on me should the investment fail."

William lifted the mug to his mouth. But he barely wet his lips with the liquid. "The investment did fail—quite spectacularly. My father shot himself. And his *friend*—" he drew that last word out, a curl to his lip "—thought that a promise made to a man who killed himself was no promise at all. What little property remained was forfeit when my father was adjudged a suicide. And so down I went to London, to try and make shift for myself."

"Where did all this take place?"

"Leicester. I still have the edge of their speech on my tongue. I've tried to eradicate it, but…"

He looked down, moving his cup in gentle circles. Perhaps he was trying to read his own tea leaves. More likely, Lavinia thought, he was avoiding her gaze.

"So you see, I am in fact the lowest of the low. I am the son of a suicide. I make a bare eighteen pounds a year. I was once a member of that unfortunate class that your lovely books label the deserving poor. After I had you—after I took to my bed a woman I could not afford to marry—I don't qualify as deserving any longer. Even if I had the coin to take you as my wife, I don't think I'd have the temerity."

Lavinia stood, the better to knock sense into his head.

But already he was setting down his tea, stepping away from her.

"It's getting on toward morning," he said. "I'd best get you home." And then he turned toward the hall and left her.

Chapter Five

WILLIAM WALKED DOWN THE HALL. He had made the matter as plain as he dared to her. She'd wanted to argue—he'd seen it in her eyes. Her words could have tied him in knots. And having to watch her deliver those arguments—having to hold his distance from her when every fiber in his being yearned toward her—had been almost impossible. But she had no way to debate straightforward gestures. He hid behind those unarguable motions now. He got his coat. He walked to the door. He opened it, and stood there in silence until she came from the kitchen.

Even then she stopped by his arm and looked up at him. Her blue eyes seemed to see right through to the contents of his soul. So what if she took the measure of that sorry item? After all, he'd set it out for her to see, a standard tattered past the point of all repair.

He walked outside, into the chill of early morning. She followed, her eyes liquid, her skin seeming to light with an incandescent glow against that mass of white fog. He wasn't sure he could bear another fifteen minutes in her presence—but whatever depths he'd plumbed, he had not sunk so far as to send a woman alone into the maw of that dampening mist. Least of all Lavinia.

Outside, Norwich Court was a silent sea of mist. Tendrils of white curled around the gaslight on the corner and combed long, thin fingers through the tangled branches of the trees. Lavinia came up behind him. He could feel the warmth of her body radiating through the fog. She was mere inches away from his embrace. She'd never felt so distant.

"I rather think," she said, "that *I* should be the one to decide if you're deserving."

He hunched his shoulders deeper and drew his coat about him. "I don't wish to speak about this at present."

"Not at present? Very well."

He was surprised—and perhaps a touch disappointed—at the grace with which she accepted his pronouncement. Silence enfolded them. They walked in darkness. William counted to thirty slowly, one number for every two steps, and then she spoke again.

"How about now, then?"

He was staring straight ahead as they walked, the better to ignore her. But there wasn't much to see on an early, foggy morning. A bakery had just come to life, the light from its windows diffusing gold through the mist. As they passed, the smell of the first baking of cinnamon-and-spice bread wafted out.

But the scent of those warm ovens was soon left behind, and there was nothing else he could focus on in the swirling fog. He felt a muscle twitch in his jaw.

"Very well," Lavinia said. "You don't need to say anything."

That muscle twitched, harder.

"I shall supply both halves of the conversation. I'm rather good at that, you know."

He had to admit, her proclamation came as no great surprise.

"Besides," she said slyly, "you're very handsome when you're taciturn."

Oh, he was not going to feel pleased. He was not going to look toward her. But damn it, he was delighted. And his head twisted toward her—until he caught himself and converted the motion into a shake of his head.

"*That* gesture," Lavinia said, "must be William Q. White for 'Dear Lord, she's given me a rabid compliment! Run away before it bites me!'"

He ruthlessly suppressed a traitorous grin.

"I shall imagine," she said, "that what you really meant to say was, 'Thank you, Lavinia.'"

William lifted his chin. He set his jaw and looked ahead.

"And that impassive, stony look," Lavinia continued, "is William Q. White for 'I must not smile, or she'll figure out precisely what I am not saying.' Really, William, is this silence the best you have to offer me on the way home? You've said all there is to say, and you have not one question to put to me?"

They were almost to her home now. William stopped walking and turned to her. He looked into her eyes—a dire mistake, as she smiled at him, and then his blood refused to do anything so sensible as flow demurely through his veins. It thundered instead, insistent and demanding. He wanted to learn the curve of her jaw, every lash on her lids. He wanted to run his hand down her cheek until he'd committed the feel of her skin to memory.

"I do have one question, Miss Spencer."

He should not have spoken. Her eyes lit with such hope. If he'd remained silent, perhaps she'd have realized he had nothing to give her—nothing but his eighteen pounds a year. And even that was subject to the arbitrary and rather capricious whims of Lord Blakely.

But instead, her lips curled upward in anticipation. "Ask. Oh, do ask."

He ought not. He should not dare. But he did.

"Why do you call me William Q. White?"

Her eyes widened. Her mouth opened in discomfited surprise. Clearly, she'd not been imagining anything along those lines. "Oh," she said on an inrush of breath. "I know it's too familiar. You've never actually given me permission. I ought to call you Mr. White. But I thought, perhaps, after—you know—the formality seemed somehow wrong, after we—after we—after we—" She paused, took a deep breath as if for courage, and then said the words aloud. "After we shared a bed."

Good God. She thought he was objecting to the use of his Christian name? "Don't be ridiculous."

"Oh," she said. "I know I sound mad. Completely *mad*. I can't help but be a little mad when you're looking down at me. You make me feel foolish, right to the bottom of my toes."

William ruthlessly suppressed the thrill that ran through him at her words.

"It is not the familiarity I object to," he said slowly. "I am rather more curious as to why you persist in placing a Q in the middle."

"Because I don't know what the Q stands for. Quincy?"

He must have looked as baffled as he felt, because she forged bravely onward.

"Quackenbush? Quintus? Come, you must tell me."

Finally he managed to put words to his befuddlement. "What *Q?*"

"Your middle initial. What other Q would possibly come between William and White?"

He blinked at her in continued bewilderment. "But I don't have a middle initial."

"Yes, you do. When you first applied for a subscription, I asked your name, and you told me, William Q. White. I may be a little giddy, and perhaps I might lose my head when you look at me, but I could not have manufactured such a thing out of whole cloth."

A memory asserted itself. He'd saved two years to make the initial fee for the subscription. When he'd walked into Spencer's library on High Holborn, he'd thought of nothing but books and self-improvement. And then he'd seen her, lush and lovely and briskly competent. He had suddenly known—he would be reading a great deal more than he had imagined. He'd been quite stupid that day.

Well. He'd never really stopped.

"Ah. I had forgotten. *That* Q." He smiled, faintly, and looked away.

"No, no. You cannot keep silent. You must tell me about the *Q*. I am all ears."

He glanced back at her. "All ears? No. You're a good proportion mouth." The grin he gave her slid so easily onto his face. "When I first applied for a subscription you asked my name. And I said, 'William White.'"

"No, you—"

He held up a hand. "Yes, I did. And *you* didn't even look up at me. You sat there, nib to paper, and you said, 'William White. Is that all?'" He folded his arms and gave her a firm nod.

Now it was her turn to frown in perplexity, as if his explanation were somehow insufficient.

"So you made up a middle initial rather than simply saying yes." Lavinia frowned. "The only thing I gather is that I am not mad. You are."

"Absolutely." His voice was low. "Have you any idea what a declaration of war those words are? You're a lovely woman. You can't just look at a man and ask, 'Is that all?' Any man worth his salt can give only one answer. 'Is that all?' 'No, damn it. There's more. There's *much* more.'"

She laughed with delight. "Mr. William Q. White," she said, wagging a finger, "you sly devil. I've been wanting to know the more ever since."

They were almost to her home, and William could not help but wish he could tease that laughter out of her every day. He held up his hands as if he could ward off their shared happiness.

"But, Lavinia," he said, "there will be no more. I can never make it up to you, this debt that lies between us. You have already given me more than I can repay."

The smile on her face faded into nothingness. "Is that how you see matters between us, then? As some sort of grim commerce, where the transactions are ones of personal worth and desert?"

"I took your virginity," he said baldly. "I took it, believing you had no choice—"

"Oh!" She reared back and kicked him in the leg.

He barely felt it—she'd not been aiming to hurt him—but she hopped briefly on one foot as if her own toes stung with the blow.

"No choice? Even if the promissory note had been real and enforceable, I had a choice. I could have pawned my mother's wedding ring for the funds. I could have let James take his chances with the magistrate and debtor's prison. I could have married another man—I've had offers, you know, from well-to-do gentlemen who wouldn't blink at paying ten pounds in pin money. Do not think me such a poor creature as to be confined so easily without choice. I chose you, and I would choose you again and again and again."

It was sheer torture to hear those words, to look into those blazing eyes and not take her in his arms.

"And, as we are speaking of debts," she said grimly, "what of *my* debt to *you?*"

"What debt?

"Ten pounds. You paid *ten pounds* to save me from having to choose between those unpalatable options. And do not tell me you did it to force me into your bed—because you and I both know that if I had said no, you would never have enforced the note. I am deeply in your debt."

"You're talking nonsense. It's nothing."

"Nothing? Bread with no butter? Tea, persuaded to give up its flavor seven or eight times? Don't tell me ten pounds means nothing to you, William. I know you better than that. Tell me—with all the uses to which you could have put that windfall, did you even hesitate to dedicate it to my service?"

"It certainly doesn't signify," he continued. "Mere money, in comparison with what you've given me."

"So it's nonsense, what I owe you. But what you owe me is a tremendous burden, one that can never be repaid? Love is not about accounting. It's not lines on a ledger. You cannot store up credit and redeem yourself at some later date, not with gifts or deeds or any number of coins, no matter how carefully you bestow them. You repay love with love, William."

She watched him expectantly. All he had to do was move forward into the space she claimed. His hands would find hers; her lips would naturally lift to his. And she would be his. His partner—but in this game of better or worse, and sickness or health, all he could offer her was poorer and poorer and yet poorer again.

If she'd built an unstable house around the two of them out of romantic notions, it was best to kick it to twigs quickly.

"It's nonsense," he said. "It's nonsense because I don't love you." He forced himself to look in her eyes, to take in the hurt spread across her face. Her pain, her rejection of him, would be his just reward. But better to hurt her once than to drag her into joint misery with him.

But she did not flinch away. Her eyes did not cloud with tears. Instead, she shook her head, very slowly. A shiver ran down William's spine. She stretched up on tiptoes and set her hands on his forearms. Her warm mouth pursed a finger's breadth from his. It would take her only an instant to place those soft lips against his. And if she did—if she kissed him now—she'd recognize his words for the obvious lies they were.

"William," she said softly. Her breath was the sweetest cinnamon against his lips. "Do you think me such a goose as to believe your idiotic assertions, after all this?"

"Oh?" The word was all he could manage—one syllable, trying to breathe a world of distance between them.

"Oh," she said with great finality. "You are hopelessly in love with me."

He'd tried to run. He'd tried to keep himself from that realization. But she pronounced sentence upon him as a matter of fact, as if she were reading the price of cotton from the morning paper. And she was right. He could not admit it, not aloud. Instead, he leaned down and rested his forehead against hers in tacit acknowledgment. *Yes. I am hopelessly in love with you.*

It didn't change anything.

She stepped back and let go of his arms. He felt her departure like a palpable blow to his gut.

"As it turns out," she said quietly, "I haven't any use for hopelessness."

He couldn't have her. Still, her rejection felt as if she'd kicked him not on the leg, but rather higher.

"Lavinia, I dare not—"

"Dare," she said, her voice shaking. "That's a command, William. *Dare.* Hope. If you won't accept my gift, I won't accept yours. And you really, *really*, do not want to know what I shall have to do to come up with ten pounds."

And with that, she turned and walked into her family's circulating library.

⌘ ⌘ ⌘

EVEN THOUGH IT FELT as if three days had passed, it was still early morning when Lavinia came quietly up the stairs. She came as she'd left, her quilted half boots in her hand. But when she reached the top landing, she discovered she was not alone. James sat, awake and dressed, at the kitchen table. He watched her come into the room, watched as she hung her cloak on a peg and set her footgear on the floor. He didn't ask where she'd been. He did not accuse her of anything. He didn't need to; she accused herself.

She felt adrift. Her gaze skittered across the room and fell on the books where she'd kept the family accounts. How many times had she stared at those figures? How many times had she wanted to make them right, hoped that if they were correct, that everything would come out?

She'd imagined herself saving enough pennies so she could pick out a scarf for James—something soft and warm. She'd wanted to swaddle him up and keep him safe. But she'd held him so tightly he'd never learned to do for himself.

Instead of giving him safety, she'd handed him powerlessness. Instead of gifting him with stability, she'd robbed him of the capacity to survive in rough seas. She'd smothered him with competent, loving efficiency.

Lavinia swallowed a lump in her throat and walked across the room, away from James. She'd left the account books open on the desk last night. Careful entries on the page looked up at her. Hadn't she just said it?

Love is not lines on a ledger. You repay love with love.

She shut the books gently and placed the smaller atop the larger. Even now, it bothered her that the two ledgers were of slightly different sizes, and so could not be aligned properly. She gathered them in her arms, uneven though the stack was, and walked across the room to where James sat.

He didn't say anything. She sat down next to him and placed the heavy volumes on the table.

Still he didn't open his mouth.

Finally, Lavinia let go of the doubts bedeviling her heart and pushed the books across the table toward him. "Here," she said abruptly.

It turned out, her brother was not the only one who spoke a foreign tongue. A stranger off the street might have thought she was giving her brother so much bound paper. But she knew without even asking that James had understood precisely what she'd just said.

I was wrong. You were right. I'm sorry. I trust you.

She'd once heard a Scotsman boast that up north, they had a hundred words for rain. Mizzle clung to coats in wet, foggy mists; rain dribbled down. On dismal, dreich days water fell in plowtery showers. When liquid falling from the sky was all the weather you had, you manufactured a lot of words to capture its nuance.

Maybe there was no language of Younger Brother or Older Sister. There was only a language of families, a tongue woven from a lifetime of shared experiences. Its vocabulary consisted of gestures and curt sentences, incomprehensible to all outsiders. Inside, it wasn't difficult to translate at all.

I love you.

James didn't say a word in response. Instead, he put his arm around her and pulled her close. She ruffled his hair. A hundred awkward and unwieldy words, all coming down to the same thing after all: *I love you.*

⌘　⌘　⌘

WILLIAM HAD THOUGHT he'd made up his mind to refuse Mr. Sherrod's solicitor. But Lavinia had dared him to hope. If she was willing to forgive a black stain on his honor, ought he not be prepared to swallow a little oiliness in exchange?

He'd met the man at first light, early on Christmas Eve. They'd had an appointment in a dingy upstairs office, just off Fleet Street. The solicitor had dressed for their morning appointment with sartorial stupidity. He wore a ghastly waistcoat of red-striped purple—or was it purple-striped red?—paired with a jacket and trousers in a cheap, shiny blue fabric. An ostentatious gold-headed cane leaned against his chair.

"Right," the solicitor said, shuffling a pile of papers on his desk. His tone was all brisk business. "I assume we've come to an understanding, then. You'll file for relief in Chancery, contesting Mr. Sherrod's will on the grounds of insanity. I will protest, saying that the foibles of his mind were precisely what one might expect in a man of his age."

"And then I'll get the money?" Two weeks ago, five thousand pounds might have meant surcease from drudgery, an escape from his cold world. It would have meant hot fires and fresh meat and large, comfortable rooms. Today, he could think of only one thing he wanted. Five thousand pounds meant Lavinia. It meant he could ask her to marry him, selfish idiot that he was. He could lift his eyes to her face. He could offer her everything she deserved— riches and wealth, without any hint of privation. She would have everything of the best.

No. Not everything. The man that came with it would not be up to her standards.

"Well," the solicitor hedged, "you might not get the money *immediately*. You might have to wait until after Chancery has sorted matters out, after it has conducted a hearing or…or two on the matter. But surely then, you'll have his fortune."

She would want him to grasp at any chance for her. Wouldn't she? Wouldn't she want a man who was able to hope?

William swallowed the bitter taste in his mouth. "What would I have to tell the courts?"

"Simple. Tell them Mr. Sherrod was mad. Manufacture stories, explaining that he saw things that were not present, that he spoke to pixies. Find folk who would attest to such tales. It would be a simple matter, if you paid—ahem, I mean, if you found enough of them."

"You expect me to lie, then."

"Goodness. I would never suborn perjury. I want you to tell the truth." This supercilious speech was somewhat weakened by a wink. "The truth, and nothing but the truth. A hint of embroidery, though, would not be amiss. Think of a court case like a woman's frock—you hide the parts of the figure that are not so flattering, and frame the bosom so that everyone can look at the enticing bits." The solicitor made a gesture in the direction of his own chest. "Just enough embellishment to convince the court of your claim, hmm?"

No matter what this greasy lawyer told him, William was fairly certain he had nothing but a tiny chance at success. He might not find people to testify. The court might not believe them. Sherrod's widow would undoubtedly claim otherwise. Still, a tiny chance was a chance nonetheless.

Was this hope that he felt, this grim determination to see the task through? Was it hope that wrapped around his throat, choking him like a noose? Was that morass, sinking like a stone in his stomach as he gritted his teeth and prepared to do business with this oily man, what he needed to accept?

Yes.

He opened his mouth to give his assent.

But as he did, he heard that voice again.

You don't have to do this.

The voice was wrong. He did have to do this. Today, when he went in to work, he might lose everything. He might have no position, and Lavinia could be pregnant. He *had* to accept any chance, no matter how small, that could help.

No, you don't. You don't have to do this.

This time, he recognized the words for what they were. They didn't come from some outside agency. He was the speaker. Even if he denied it—even as he betrayed himself—he'd always retained some semblance of his honor. It had not disappeared. It had simply been here, waiting for him to follow.

For so long, he'd simply believed he had sunk so low in society that he did not dare to lift his face. Oh, yes, he'd dishonored himself. But he couldn't find honor by seeking forgiveness. He could not wait for Lavinia or anyone else to absolve him of his sins.

If William ever hoped to have some measure of honor, he had to be an honorable man.

The solicitor must have seen his hesitation.

"Think," he said, "on the *revenge* you could take on the man who destroyed your father."

He'd dwelled on that dark thought for a decade. But how could he expect forgiveness for his own sins, if he could not grant absolution to the man who'd wronged him?

He would have to give up any chance at those five thousand pounds. That meant he would give up any chance at having Lavinia—but then, when Lavinia had told him to hope, she hadn't meant that he should hope for her.

She'd wanted him to hope for himself.

"No," he said. It felt good in every way to know that he could choose to be honorable, even knowing the cost.

Confusion lit the solicitor's face. "No? What could you possibly mean by no?"

"No, I won't embellish the truth past recognition. No, I won't tell lies. No, I won't seek revenge to keep you in Chancery fees. I'm not that kind of man." He had been, once, but he was no longer.

"Who will ever know that you lied?"

William shrugged. "Me?"

"You?" The solicitor laughed in scorn. "Well, trust in yourself, then. You'll not deliver yourself from poverty."

William stood. He'd thought his soul had depreciated until it was worth less than nothing. Strange he'd not realized: it always had precisely the value he chose to give it.

As he left, the man called out after him. "I hope you take great pleasure in yourself. Likely it's all you'll ever have."

The words no longer sounded like the curse they once would have been.

⌘　⌘　⌘

ON CHRISTMAS EVE MORNING, Lavinia shared the responsibility of running the shop with her brother. The two of them, even in that small downstairs room, should not have made the room feel so close. Yes, there were nearly fifteen hundred volumes packed into a tiny space. The shelves stretched head height and above. But Lavinia had never found the two tiny rooms confining before, not even with a surfeit of customers. But today the books seemed to tower over her, choking her with memories.

She would look up from her desk and remember the first time she'd seen William, standing so ill at ease in front of her, asking for a subscription. She would place a volume back on the shelf and remember the sight of him in that very spot, searching for a title. He would run his finger carefully down a leather binding. In those days, she'd envied the books. But now, he'd touched her with greater reverence.

He'd not been able to hide the meaning of those gestures. Over and over, he'd told her he loved her. He loved her, and so he made her wretchedly watered-down tea. He loved her and he longed to touch her, but instead he warned her she'd have no butter with her bread. He loved her.

And yet she'd brought him hopelessness rather than happiness. Together, they'd managed to share a fine portion of guilt. She might gladly have suffered deprivation for him, but he was not the kind of man who could watch the woman he loved be deprived.

Over at the small table near the door, Lavinia watched as James entered a book loan in the ledger. He slipped two pennies in the cash box and then wrapped a book and waved farewell to Mr. Bellow. As he recorded the transaction, he avoided her gaze. She came up to the table anyway, approaching it from the front, as if she were a customer instead of a fellow laborer. Still, he winced.

"I did it exactly as you instructed," he whispered. "Did I do it wrong? Oh God, I did it so completely backward you can tell it's wrong without even reading what I've entered." He put his head in his hands.

"You're doing very well." She resisted the urge to turn the book upside down to check. "Perfect, even." No, she was not going to even glance down. "You're doing so well, in fact, that I am going upstairs to rest."

He lifted his face. His eyes shone in pleasure. "I'll take care of everything." Then he paused. "But perhaps an hour or two before we close up the shop, would you be willing to take over again? There is one thing I should like to take care of this evening."

She patted her brother's hand. "Of course," she said with a smile.

She headed upstairs. She would not have minded deprivation for herself. But William… If her gloves had holes, William's hands would freeze in sympathy. If she ate brown, unbuttered bread, the bitter taste would linger on his palate.

She'd given him hopelessness. She'd made him miserable. If she truly loved him, perhaps she needed to let him go.

Chapter Six

TWENTY-FOUR HOURS EARLIER, William had cowered in the office where he worked, for fear of losing his position. Today when he walked in, he felt not even a hint of disquietude.

Why had he been so afraid? He was young. He was competent. And even if he were turned off, he would find something else. Losing a position where he was regularly treated like the grimiest gutter refuse was not something to fear. It was something to celebrate.

When the door to the office opened just after nine and in walked Lord Blakely followed by his glowering grandson, William felt triumph.

When he was let go, it would be a financial setback. It might take weeks to find work again; his wages might even be reduced. He ought to have been terrified. But this was not a punishment, to be allowed to walk out of this dark and dismal place. It was an opportunity.

The two lords stepped into the back office. After a few minutes Mr. Dunning walked up to William and whispered that he'd been asked to enter the room.

They were unlikely to be inviting him to a picnic lunch. Just before he stood, Mr. Dunning laid his hand on William's shoulder—an empty gesture of pointless support.

William smiled and stood, calm. *Let them sack me. Please.*

He'd expected the back office to appear precisely as he'd left it yesterday.

But when he arrived, there had been one tiny alteration. Lord Blakely still peered at him from beneath white, bushy eyebrows, examining him as if he were some strange insect. But the marquess had not seated himself in his throne behind the desk. Instead, he'd ensconced his grandson in the position of power. Lord Wyndleton sat, ill at ease. He smoldered with a repressed anger so fierce that William thought he would leave scorch marks where he tapped his fingers against the desk.

Three account books, a small portion of the work William had done over his years of employment, made a small pile on the edge of the desk.

The old marquess picked up one negligently and thumbed through the pages. "Sometime between the months of January and—" a pause, and a last glance at the end of the third book "—April, Bill Blight here made a mistake."

William did not mind being stripped of his position and his wages. He no longer fancied losing his dignity alongside. "My lord, my name is William White."

Naturally, Lord Blakely took no notice of the interjection. "Bill Blight made an error. Find it and then sack him. When you can lay the mistake before me, I shall allow you to leave."

Lord Wyndleton sighed heavily, but reached for a book. He opened it and stared intently at the first page. His grandfather watched, silent, for a few minutes as the young lord scanned the entries. Finally he shook his head and walked out, leaving the two younger men together. William heard the front door to the building rattle shut; shortly after, the jingle of his carriage sounded.

As soon as they were alone, the young lord looked up. "Did you make a mistake between the months of January and April?"

William rolled his eyes. "Yes."

"Well, tell me what it was. I haven't got all day."

"I don't know. Between the months of January and April, I must have accounted for upward of four thousand transactions. Of course there was a mistake somewhere in the lot—it's impossible not to make one. If your grandfather were even halfway rational, he wouldn't sack his employees for minor imperfections."

William had thought the insult to the marquess would be enough to have him sent on his way.

"Hmm," Lord Wyndleton said. "Four thousand transactions." He glanced up at William, and then shook his head as if it were somehow William's fault he'd been so efficient. "What a bloody nuisance."

With that, the man turned his head down to the books. Minutes passed. His eyes moved slowly down column after column. He turned one page, then another. At the turn of the tenth page, William sighed and sat down without permission.

The old marquess might have turned him off for that offense in an instant; his grandson didn't even appear to notice.

At the twentieth page, William began to wish he hadn't been so meticulous in his accounting. If he'd missed a shilling on the first page, at least he would have been able to leave.

At the twenty-sixth page, Lord Wyndleton sighed loudly. "I bloody hate this," he muttered.

How sweet. They had something in common. It was time to escalate his plan to get sacked.

William was already bored. And he had nothing to lose. "I hear you are interested in scientific pursuit."

Lord Wyndleton's eyes moved only to glance down the page of numbers in front of him. He turned his hand over. It might have been an unconscious gesture. It might have been the barest acknowledgment of William's uttered words.

William decided to take it as acknowledgment. "Well, then. I should think you'd enjoy numbers."

Lord Wyndleton shrugged but still did not look up. He flipped to the front of the book, then back to page twenty-six. For a long while William thought the man was going to ignore him.

But the viscount finally spoke without lifting his eyes from the page. "I do like numbers. I like numbers when they are attached to little *t* and double-dot-*x*. Maybe a calculation of probability." He spoke in swift, clipped tones, his voice unemotional and unvarying. "I dislike arithmetic. Finance bores me. It has no rules to discover. Just opportunity for error."

"Ah," William said. "You prefer calculus?"

Lord Wyndleton sighed and turned to page twenty-seven. Then he looked up—although he didn't look directly at William. Instead, he leaned his head back and fixed his gaze on the ceiling. "Let me tell you what I *dislike*. I dislike servants who make obscure mistakes, forcing me to spend Christmas Eve morn studying dusty accounting tomes. My dislike accelerates when said servant attempts to distract me from my duty by yammering on. That means, *Bill*, I dislike you."

"That," said William, "makes us a pair. I despise men who let their vast fortunes go to waste. You're so helpless, you can't even get thirty miles on a Christmas Eve. You're spending your morning glowering at books instead of going to Tattersall's and purchasing a very swift horse."

"If my grandfather did not control my fortune, I would have done precisely that."

The viscount was angry. He was, also, William realized, entirely serious.

William stared at him for a few moments, his own pique dissipating. "You really don't like finance," he finally said. "Your grandfather doesn't control your fortune."

"Ha." Lord Wyndleton undoubtedly intended that single syllable to be a dismissal.

"It wasn't I who made the mistake. It was the marquess."

"Do be quiet."

"He ought never have left you alone with me."

Lord Wyndleton slammed his pen down. "Oh, Lord almighty," he muttered to the desktop. "What are you going to do to me? Annoy me to death?"

"You see," William continued, "I've recorded the accounting for your trust every month since I started here. Those funds became yours, free and clear, upon your majority."

Viscount Wyndleton cocked his head and turned it. It was a gesture reminiscent of his grandfather—and yet on him, it seemed attentive rather than predatory. His eyes were steady and almost golden-brown. For a few seconds he stared at William, his lips parted.

William knew precisely what that look meant. He was entertaining hopes. Then he let out a breath and shook his head. "No. When the trust was established, the money would have become mine on my majority. But six years ago I came to an agreement with my grandfather. I signed over control of my funds after my majority. In exchange he let me—well, never mind that. Your information is wrong."

He paused, tapping his pen against his wrist. "Next time, if you have something to say, come out and say it. I don't hold with talking in such a roundabout fashion, as if you're a cat circling your prey. Pounce already and be done with it."

For a second William thought the young lord intended to leave his words at a rebuke. But then Lord Wyndleton looked up again. "But thank you," he said. "It was well-meant."

So the grandson was not the grandfather, however alike they might have seemed at first. What had started as resentment on William's part had turned into something—something more. He wasn't sure what it was yet.

William stood. "I've seen the statements. I've recorded the accounts. I know every detail, and they're in your own name."

"Couldn't be. There must be some legal nicety you're missing. Blakely is too meticulous. I signed a contract, and I have no doubt the matter it covered was executed immediately. *He* wouldn't miss the opportunity to keep me under his thumb."

"This contract—you signed it six years ago?" The hackles on William's neck rose. His calm dissipated. A great and sudden weight tensed on his shoulders. "You're two-and-twenty now?"

Lord Wyndleton waved his hand and turned back to the books, dismissing William. "This isn't getting me any closer to my mother's home."

William strode forward and slapped his hand over the page Lord Wyndleton was reading. "I'm pouncing. The agreement wasn't executed because it couldn't have been. Legally you were an infant. The contract was a nullity. It's the rankest abuse of power for your guardian to have required you to give away what was rightfully yours in exchange for…for something else that is rightfully yours."

Lord Wyndleton let out his breath, slowly. "Are you sure?"

"I can prove it," William said. "Tell them you need to verify my figures against another set of books. They won't deny you."

A curt nod, and William left the room. Forty-five minutes later, with the books spread out in front of him, Lord Wyndleton believed. He looked up.

"Aren't you some kind of lowly clerk or some such? How do you know arcane details about the legalities of contracts?"

William smiled faintly. *I made love to a beautiful woman* hardly seemed to be an answer that would keep him in his lordship's good graces. "I read," he finally said. It was true. Just not the whole truth. "I've been training myself to take over an estate."

"Expectations?"

"No, my lord. None. Just…" William nodded once. "Just hopes, really."

Lord Wyndleton drummed his fingers against the desk. "If I had my way," he said quietly, "I'd leave England entirely. I've wanted to explore the Americas—but lacking funds, of course, it's never been an option. It is now. But I need someone here. He would have to be someone who could be trusted to make sure my funds arrived wherever I had need of them. Someone who could not be suborned by my grandfather. Someone competent and efficient—perhaps even someone who likes finance—even if he does make the occasional mistake sometime between the months of January and April. Now—" Lord Wyndleton leaned back and looked at the ceiling "—if only I knew someone like that."

The viscount was curt, rude and demanding. But he was not a tyrant like his grandfather. And he was fundamentally fair in a way that the marquess had not been. William shrugged. "And here I thought you didn't like roundaboutation."

"Well," Lord Wyndleton said, "are you in need of a position?"

"As it happens, yes. Although I regret to inform you, my previous employer is not likely to speak highly of my character, as I helped his grandson uncover the secret of his financial independence. It was a shocking lapse of judgment on my part."

Lord Wyndleton pursed his lips and nodded. "A shocking lapse. Can I trust you, Mr. White?"

"Of course you can," William said, holding his breath. "You're going to pay me seventy-five pounds a year."

The viscount leaned back in his chair. "I am?"

William had chosen the salary to be deliberately, obscenely high. He'd had no doubts his lordship would argue him down to a reasonable thirty—perhaps forty—pounds. Forty pounds. On forty pounds, a man might rent decent quarters for himself and a wife. He might have children without worrying about whether he could provide for them. Forty pounds a year meant Lavinia. He was about to open his mouth to lower his demand when the young lord spoke again.

"Seventy-five pounds a year." Lord Wyndleton sounded distinctly amused. "Is that supposed to be a lot of money?"

"You're joking. God, yes."

His lordship waved a hand negligently. "My mother and sister live in Aldershot. If you are good enough to get me out of London before my grandfather notices," he said quietly, "I'll treble that."

He stood as William stared after him in shock.

"Come along," he said. "I believe you have your resignation to tender."

⌘ ⌘ ⌘

BY TWO IN THE AFTERNOON, William and his new employer had barred the old marquess from his grandson's personal finances. The viscount's first purchase had been a coach and four. They'd obtained money for changes, and his new employer had been on his way. William went to Spencer's circulating library.

He made it there by three. The building was lit with a dim glow; the door, when he tried it, was unlocked. Good. She hadn't yet closed the shop for Christmas Eve.

He opened the door. She was sitting at her stool again, winding a strand of hair through her fingers. Up. Down. Soon those would be his fingers there, stroking her hair. Rubbing her cheek. There was a thread of melancholy to her movements.

She glanced up and saw him, but her face did not light. Instead, it shuttered in on itself. Lavinia, the woman who smiled at everyone who entered her shop, pressed her lips together and looked away. It was not the best of beginnings.

William advanced on her.

She spoke first. "I have a Christmas gift for you." Still she kept her eyes on the desk in front of her. Her hands lay on the table—pressed flat against that solid surface, not relaxed and curved. Her fingertips were white.

"I don't want a gift, Lavinia."

Still she didn't look at him. Instead she pulled open a drawer—the quiet protest of wood against wood sounded—and she rummaged inside. When she found whatever it was she was looking for, she lobbed it in his direction. As she still hadn't looked at him, her aim was poor. He stretched to catch what she'd thrown. It was a pouch barely the size of his hand. The container was light. It might well have been empty.

"I told you," she said quietly, her eyes still on her hands. "I told you, you wouldn't want to know what I would have to do to pay back your ten pounds." Her voice was small.

His heart stopped. "I don't want ten pounds from you."

Finally she lifted her chin to look in his eyes. "I know," she whispered. "But I want you to have it."

There was the faintest tinge of red at the corner of her eyes. His hand contracted around the fabric. She'd had options. But William's original ten pounds had disappeared. That left…No. She couldn't have agreed to marry another man. She wouldn't have.

Would she? She sat, pale and stricken. She looked miserable.

"Don't do it, Lavinia," he warned. "Choose me. I came here to tell you—you wanted me to find hope. I've found another position, a better one. I can afford you now."

She jerked back as if she'd been slapped. "You can *afford* me, William? You coerce me to your bed. You lie to me and say you don't love me. And you think I was waiting for you to gather the coin to purchase me?"

William bit his lip. If he'd been a better man—if he'd been worthy of her from the start—if he hadn't coerced her into intercourse, and then hurt her to drive her away from him not once, but *twice*—perhaps he might have had her. He'd as good as told her to give up hope this morning. Now she had.

"I'm sorry," he said simply.

She raised her chin. "I never wanted your apology."

"I know," William said. "It's all I have."

She didn't say anything. Instead, she bit her lip and looked away. Once, he'd tried to steal her choice back from her. He'd not do it a second time. He let out a deep breath.

"Merry Christmas, Lavinia," he whispered.

Somehow he managed to find the door. Somehow he managed to wrest it open and walk through it with some semblance of grace. He even managed to stumble down the street. Halfway to the crossroads he realized he was still holding that damned bag she'd thrown at him, with its ten bloody pounds. He balled it up in his hand and squeezed in frustration—and stood still.

If he had bothered to think about such a thing, he would have supposed that the sack felt light and deflated because it contained a single bank note, folded into quarters. But instead of the crisp, malleable shape of a paper rectangle he felt a single circle press against his palm.

A circle? There was no such thing as a ten-pound coin. Besides, he realized as he ran his hands over the cloth, coins were not hollow in the middle. And this one was barely the diameter of a sixpence, but three times as thick.

Breath held, he opened the pouch and pulled out the object inside. It was a plain, round circle of gold— a ring too dainty to ever be intended for a man's finger. He stared at it in frozen wonder. She'd had other choices besides marrying another man. *I could have pawned my mother's wedding ring.*

But she hadn't pawned it. She'd given it to him.

⌘ ⌘ ⌘

LAVINIA HAD WATCHED THE DOOR where William had left.

Her choices were few. Should she humiliate herself and run after him? Should she at least wait a decent amount of time before hunting him down and making him pay in kisses? Or should she kick the desk in frustration and give up on Mr. William Q. White ever figuring out how to express the concept of love without reference to funds?

Lavinia sat down at her desk and put her head in her hands. She didn't dare cry—not now, not when she needed to head upstairs to see her father. It was Christmas Eve and tonight the family needed to laugh. She needed to pretend Christmas had come without mulling wine or roasting goose. What she didn't need to do was cry over the man's sheer perversity.

The bell rang.

The door opened.

Lavinia lifted her head from her hands. Her heart turned over. William stood, framed by the doorway against the dark of the night. Little wisps of snow covered his collar and kissed the brim of his hat. He took off his coat, folding it and setting it on the low table to his right. Then he turned and shut the door. She heard the snick of a key turning in the lock, and she swallowed. He did not say anything, but he drank her in, top to bottom, his eyes running languidly down her form.

"Does that door behind you lock, as well?"

She shook her head.

"Pity." He lifted a chair off the floor and strode past her.

"What are you doing?"

"I'm rearranging your furniture." He tilted the chair at an angle and wedged it under the door handle.

"There. This time we shan't be bothered by intruding little brothers." He turned to her. She was still seated on her stool. Her toes curled in her slippers as he walked forward. He towered before her. Then he bent and picked her up. His arms around her were warm and strong.

The doors were barred, so nobody could save her. For that matter, with the books piled in front of the one tiny window, nobody could see her. Thank God. She melted into his arms.

He straightened. But she had only a few bare seconds of his warm embrace before he set her on the desk. He did not move away from her. Her thighs parted, and he stepped between her legs. She was still looking into his eyes. He rested his forehead against hers, and she shut her eyes.

"I collect," William said, his hand reaching up to cup her cheek, "that you want me to give your ring back."

She opened her mouth to answer, but all that came from her vocal cords was a pointless squeak. Instead she nodded.

"You can't have it." His eyes bored into her. His fingers whispered down the line of her jaw, to rest against her chin. He tipped her head back.

"You can't have it," he repeated, "unless you wear it for me."

She nodded again.

"I also collect," he said, "that when I came in, I should have said something rather more like—"

He leaned forward.

"Like?" she prodded.

His lips touched hers.

He tasted like cinnamon and cloves, like the Christmas she no longer dreaded facing. His lips roamed over hers, tasting, testing. His hands slid from her jaw down to her waist. And she was touching him, his shoulders pulling the hard length of his body against hers. She was catching fire, yearning to consume him. Her hands ran through his silky hair, pulling his head toward hers. But however intimate the touch of his tongue against hers, however insistent the press of his hard erection through the layers of her skirts, his hands remained virtuously clasped on her waist.

He pulled away from her. She'd rearranged his hair into a tangled and adorable mess.

"Well," he murmured, smiling at her.

"Mr. William Q. White," Lavinia said, "I should like to know your intentions."

"I intend to love you as you deserve."

"That is a good start. I should like to be loved more, however."

He leaned in and kissed her again, a sweet touch of his lips, when she wanted heat.

"But you asked for my intentions. You must know I intend to ask your father's permission to call the banns."

Close to him as she was, his hands still on her waist, she felt a subtle tension fill his body, as if he were wary of her response. As if *she* had not asked him to marry her already.

Lavinia clucked and shook her head. That wariness grew, and he pulled away from her ever so subtly. She reached up to touch his cheek. His skin was rough with evening stubble. "Do not tell me you barred the door just so that you could steal a mere kiss. Really, William. Is that all?"

A slow smile spread across his face. His hands pressed against her waist and then slid lower, the heat of his palms burning into her hips.

"Is that all?" he echoed. "No, damn it." His hands inched down to her thighs. "There's more. There's *much* more."

And then his lips fell on hers again. This time, he exercised no restraint. His body pressed hers. His hands pulled her against him. He kissed down her neck; she threw back her head and let his tongue trail fire along her skin. She felt his warm lips trace her collarbone. He breathed heat against the neckline of her dress. And then he was rearranging her bodice, tugging, persuading, until he caught her breast in his mouth.

A sharp swirl of excitement filled her. But his touch didn't satisfy her. Instead, it only whetted her hunger. His other hand was on her ankle now, lifting her legs to one side, pushing her skirts up. His fingers fluttered against her damp sex.

Pleasure twined with want.

She desired—she needed—she *required*. And what she needed she couldn't have said, except more, damn it, more. But he knew. His body was hard against hers. He fumbled with his breeches—and then he filled her, hard and thick and long.

His hands braced against the desk; her legs wrapped around his waist. And then she could think of nothing but the heat of his skin against hers, the thrust of his body inside hers, his hand on her breast, his lips on her mouth. And then even these thoughts were ripped away from her as she gave herself up to him.

Afterward, her body still throbbing with delicious satiety, his hair slightly damp and spiking from his exertions, he held her close. His breath was warm against her cheek.

"I am," he said in her ear, "completely, utterly and devotedly yours. If you will have me."

She leaned her forehead against his chest. "I suppose I shall." His arms were around her shoulders now, his hands caressing her. She inhaled. He smelled of starch, of salt, and of…of burning cloves?

Lavinia pulled back and sniffed the air in puzzlement. A complex, bitter scent had wound its way into the room. It had just the faintest hint of sulfur to it. But the disturbing smell did not waft from William. Instead, it was coming from upstairs.

Lavinia disentangled herself from his embrace. She jumped off the table and patted her gown into place. Quickly she bounded across the room and yanked the chair from its spot under the door handle.

She was running up the stairs, her footfalls heavy, before she could even imagine what was going on.

Her brother stood by the hob, his hands full of heavy cloth. He held a pot that emitted clouds of dark steam.

"Ah," James said with a smile. "Lavinia. I'm mulling wine."

"Wine? Where did you get wine? How did you purchase the spices?" And then, seeing what sat on the table, Lavinia gave a little shriek. "A goose? However did you obtain a goose?"

James shrugged. "I sold mother's pearl pendant. She gave it to me, and I thought...well, I thought she would want us to have this." He shrugged, and then continued brightly. "Besides, what with my making mistakes in the shop, and your getting married, we could use a little extra money now."

Behind her, Lavinia could her William's footsteps as he ascended the stairs.

"How did you know I was getting married? *I* just found out."

James fixed Lavinia with his most serious look. "Next time," he said, "if you are trying to keep secrets, you might consider writing something other than 'Mrs. William Q. White' in the margin of the account books when you test your pen."

She stared at her brother, her cheeks burning in embarrassment. "James—please—he's coming up the stairs now. I haven't done that in almost a year. Don't tell him."

Her brother shook his head in gleeful amusement. William reached the upstairs landing and hesitated, as if not quite sure whether he would be welcomed into the family.

James cast one pointed glance over his shoulder to the desk where the books lay, pages spread open, telltale margin scribbles and all. But instead of teasing Lavinia further, he gestured with the pot he held in his hands. "Did you know," he asked William conversationally, "that wine can *burn?* I hadn't thought it possible, as it's a liquid—but look at this. The pot is completely scorched."

Epilogue

London, precisely thirteen years later

"MR. WHITE."

William looked up from his desk. He had served Gareth Carhart for many years now. First he'd served the Viscount Wyndleton. But in the past year the man had taken on the mantle of Lord Blakely. And William's duties had been correspondingly increased.

"A year ago," the new marquess said, "you told me you could assist with the management of the marquessate. I allowed you the chance to temporarily prove yourself."

William knew better than to interject his own commentary into the brief pause that followed. Lord Blakely disliked being interrupted, and the thread of the conversation would resume at his leisure.

"You have. Congratulations. You may consider the position, and the salary, permanent."

"Thank you, my lord." It was hardly a surprise. He'd served Lord Blakely well, and curt as the man was, he was always fair.

Another awkward pause ensued. Finally his lordship glanced at a clock. "Well?" The time showed seven past three. "Isn't it past time for you to be on your way tonight?"

In the thirteen years that William had worked for the man, he'd learned to interpret these curious pronouncements. Bad news Lord Blakely announced directly. Good news he cloaked in disdain. Outright gifts—like dismissing his man of business a full three hours early on Christmas Eve—he hid in...roundaboutation.

White stood and reached for his things. "My lord." He walked to the door. On the threshold, he paused. "My lord, if I may—"

"No," interrupted Lord Blakely. "You may not. I've no desire to hear your insincere wishes for the happiness of my Christmas."

White inclined his head. "As you wish. My lord."

Unlike his predecessor, who had descended on the hapless clerks in the Chancery Lane office like a one-man plague of locusts, the current Lord Blakely preferred that William White—his manager, man of business and otherwise facilitator of marquesslike behavior—present his reports in his Mayfair town home. He was harsh, demanding—and eminently fair. It also meant that at the end of the day, William's walk back home—now a tall town house in a respectable part of town—was substantially shortened.

As soon as he opened the door, he smelled cinnamon and citrus wafting in the air, tangled with a hint of bitter wine. But something was missing. It took him a moment to ascertain what was wrong. The house was *quiet*. It was astonishingly quiet.

He found Lavinia, sitting in a chair, twisting a lock of her hair around one finger as she read. *Not* a novel—a finance circular. A shawl, woven through with gold thread, covered her shoulders. For a long minute he watched her read. Her eyes darted intelligently across the page. Her tongue darted out to touch her finger, and she turned a page. She was, he thought, the most beautiful woman he'd ever seen.

She looked up. She did not jump or evince the least surprise that he'd arrived hours before he was expected.

"Let me guess," she said. "You conveyed my invitation to Christmas dinner to the marquess and he sacked you for the effrontery. Ah, well. It doesn't matter." She smiled at him, so he would know she was not serious. "In any event, I made more money last quarter than you, so we shall make do."

Lavinia may have been the only woman in all Christendom to invest the excess from the household accounts in railways. He walked over to stand by her.

"You also spent more money last quarter than I did," he said, laying a hand on the imported silk of her shawl. He took the excuse to stroke her shoulder.

"This? Oh, no. This was quite inexpensive. Now, tell me—am I going to have a marquess appearing at dinner tomorrow?"

"No, thank God. I did intend to ask him—truly I did—but he stopped me before I dared. It was probably for the best."

"He is the most dreadfully lonely man." She shrugged. "But I suppose it is his choice."

"Speaking of lonely. Or what is far more interesting to me, let us speak of being alone. I notice that something—or rather, some *ones* are missing."

"James has the boys. He shut the shop early today and he's taken them all out to see the Italian players."

That would explain the unearthly quiet.

"Mrs. Evans is in the kitchens. And I've sent the maids to the market. I don't believe anyone will come into the sitting room. Not for hours."

William smiled and extended his hand. "Mrs. White," he said slyly, "I think that your very expensive shawl would look far lovelier and more expensive on this floor."

Thank you!

Thanks for reading *This Wicked Gift*. I hope you enjoyed it!

- Would you like to know when my next book is available? You can sign up for my new release e-mail list at www.courtneymilan.com, follow me on twitter at @courtneymilan, or like my Facebook page at http://facebook.com/courtneymilanauthor.
- Reviews help other readers find books. I appreciate all reviews, whether positive or negative.
- *This Wicked Gift* is a prequel novella to the Carhart series. The books in the series are *Proof by Seduction* and *Trial by Desire*.

Proof by Seduction is the first full-length book in the series, and it's about Gareth Carhart, who you saw briefly in this book. If you'd like to read an excerpt from that book, please turn the page.

Excerpt: Proof by Seduction

London, April, 1838

TWELVE YEARS SPENT PLYING HER TRADE had taught Jenny Keeble to leave no part of her carefully manufactured atmosphere to chance. The sandalwood smoke wafting from the brazier added a touch of the occult: not too cloying, yet unquestionably exotic. But it was by rote that she checked the cheap black cotton draped over her rickety table; routine alone compelled her to straighten her garishly colored wall hangings.

Every detail—the cobwebs she left undisturbed in the corner of the room, the gauze that draped her basement windows and filtered the sunlight into indirect haze—whispered that here magic worked and spirits conveyed sage advice.

It was precisely the effect Jenny should have desired.

So why did she wish she could abandon this costume? True, the virulently red-and-blue-striped skirt, paired with a green blouse, did nothing to flatter her looks. Layer upon heavy layer obscured her waist and puffed her out until she resembled nothing so much as a round, multihued melon. Her skin suffocated under a heavy covering of paint and kohl. But her disquiet ran deeper than the thick lacquers of cream and powder.

A sharp rat-tat-tat sounded at the door.

She'd worked twelve years for this. Twelve years of careful lies and half truths, spent cultivating clients. But there was no room for uncertainty in Jenny's profession. She took a deep breath, and pushed Jenny Keeble's doubts aside. In her place, she constructed the imperturbable edifice of Madame Esmerelda. A woman who could see anything. Who predicted everything. And who stopped at nothing.

With her lies firmly in place, Jenny opened the door.

Two men stood on her stoop. Ned, her favorite client, she'd expected. He was awkward and lanky, as only a youth just out of adolescence could be. A shock of light brown hair topped his young features. His lips curled in an open, welcoming smile. She would have greeted him easily, but today, another fellow stood behind Ned. The stranger was extraordinarily tall, even taller than Ned. He stood several feet back, his arms folded in stern disapproval.

"Madame Esmerelda," Ned said. "I'm sorry I didn't inform you I was bringing along a guest."

Jenny peered behind Ned. The man's coat was carelessly unbuttoned. Some tailor had poured hours into the exquisite fit of that garment. It was cut close enough to the body to show off the form, but loose enough to allow movement. His sandy-brown hair was tousled, his cravat tied in the simplest of knots. The details of his wardrobe bespoke an impatient arrogance, as if his appearance was little more than a bother, his attention reserved for weightier matters.

That attention shifted to Jenny now, and a shiver raced down her spine. With one predatorial sweep of his eyes, he took in Jenny's costume from head to toe. She swallowed.

"Madame Esmerelda," Ned said, "this is my cousin."

A cold glimmer of irritation escaped the other man, and Ned expelled a feeble sigh.

"Yes, Blakely. May I present to you Madame Esmerelda." The monotone introduction wasn't even a question. "Madame, this is Blakely. That would be Gareth Carhart, Marquess of Blakely. Et cetera."

A beat of apprehension pulsed through Jenny as she curtsied. Ned had spoken of his cousin before. Based on Ned's descriptions, she'd imagined the marquess to be old and perhaps a little decrepit, obsessed with facts and figures. Ned's cousin was supposed to be coldly distant, frighteningly uncivil, and so focused on his own scientific interests that he was unaware of the people around him.

But this man wasn't distant; even standing a full yard away, her skin prickled in response to his presence. He wasn't old; he was lean without being skinny, and his cheeks were shadowed by the stubble of a man in his prime. Most of all, there was nothing unfocused about him. She'd often thought Ned had the eyes of a terrier: warm, liquid and trusting. His cousin had those of a lion: tawny, ferocious and more than a little feral.

Jenny gave silent thanks she wasn't a gazelle.

She turned and swept her arm in regal welcome. "Come in. Be seated." The men trooped in, settling on chairs that creaked under their weight. Jenny remained standing.

"Ned, how can I assist you today?"

Ned beamed at her. "Well. Blakely and I have been arguing. He doesn't think you can predict the future."

Neither did Jenny. She resented sharing that belief.

"We've agreed—he's going to use science to demonstrate the accuracy of your predictions."

"Demonstrate? Scientifically?" The words whooshed out of her, as if she'd been prodded in the stomach. Jenny grasped the table in front of her for support. "Well. That would be…" *Unlikely? Unfortunate?* "That would be unobjectionable. How shall he proceed?"

Ned waved his hand at his cousin. "Well, go ahead, Blakely. Ask her something."

Lord Blakely leaned back in his chair. Up until this moment, he had not spoken a single word; his eyes had traveled about the room, though. "You want *me* to ask her something?" He spoke slowly, drawing out each syllable with precision. "I consult logic, not old charlatans."

Ned and Jenny spoke atop each other. "She's no charlatan!" protested Ned.

But Jenny's hands had flown to her hips for another reason entirely. "Thirty," she protested, "is not old!"

Ned turned to her, his eyebrow lifting. A devastating silence cloaked the room. It was a measure of her own agitation that she'd forsaken Madame Esmerelda's character already. Instead, she'd spoken as a woman.

And the marquess noticed. That tawny gaze flicked from her kerchiefed head down to the garish skirts obscuring her waist. His vision bored through every one of her layers. The appraisal was thoroughly masculine. A sudden tremulous awareness tickled Jenny's palms.

And then he looked away. A queer quirk of his lips; the smallest exhalation, and like that, he dismissed her.

Jenny was no lady, no social match for Lord Blakely. She was not the sort who would inspire him to tip his hat if he passed her on the street. She should have been accustomed to such cursory dismissals. But beneath her skirts, she felt suddenly brittle, like a pile of dried-up potato parings, ready to blow away with one strong gust of wind. Her fingernails bit crescent moons into her hands.

Madame Esmerelda wouldn't care about this man's interest. Madame Esmerelda never let herself get angry. And so Jenny swallowed the lump in her throat and smiled mysteriously. "I am also not a charlatan."

Lord Blakely raised an eyebrow. "That remains to be proven. As I have no desire to seek answers for myself, I believe Ned will question you."

"I already have!" Ned gestured widely. "About *everything*. About *life* and *death*."

Lord Blakely rolled his eyes. No doubt he'd taken Ned's dramatic protest as youthful exaggeration. But Jenny knew it for the simple truth it was. Two years earlier, Ned had wandered into this room and asked the question that had changed both their lives: "Is there any reason I shouldn't kill myself?"

At the time, Jenny had wanted to disclaim all responsibility. Her first impulse had been to distance herself from the boy, to say she wasn't really able to see the future. But the question was not one a nineteen-year-old posed to a stranger because he was considering his options rationally. She'd known, even then, that the young man had asked because he was at his wits' end.

So she'd lied. She told him she saw happiness in his future, that he had every reason to live. He'd believed her. And as time passed, he'd gradually moved past despair. Today, he stood in front of her almost confident.

It should have counted as a triumph of some kind, a good deed chalked up to Jenny's account. But on that first day, she hadn't just taken his despair. She'd taken his money, too. And since then, she and

Ned had been bound together in this tangle of coin and deceit.

"Life and death?" Lord Blakely fingered the cheap fabric that loosely draped her chairs. "Then there should be no problem with my more prosaic proposal. I'm sure you are aware Ned must marry. Madame—Esmerelda, is it?—why don't you tell me the name of the woman he should choose."

Ned stiffened, and a chill went down Jenny's spine. Advice hidden behind spiritual maundering was one thing. But she knew that Ned had resisted wedlock, and for good reasons. She had no intention of trapping him.

"The spirits have not chosen to reveal such details," she responded smoothly.

The marquess pulled an end of lead pencil from his pocket and licked it. He bent over a notebook and scribbled a notation. "Can't predict future with particularity." He squinted at her. "This will be a damned short test of your abilities if you can do no better."

Jenny's fingers twitched in irritation. "I can say," she said slowly, "in the cosmic sense of things, he will meet her soon."

"There!" crowed Ned in triumph. "There's your specifics."

"Hmm." Lord Blakely frowned over the words he'd transcribed. "The 'cosmic sense' being something along the lines of, the cosmos is ageless? No matter which girl Ned meets, I suppose you would say he met her 'soon.' Come, Ned. Isn't she supposed to have arcane knowledge?"

Jenny pinched her lips together and turned away, her skirts swishing about her ankles. Blakely's eyes followed her; but when she cast a glance at him over her shoulder, he looked away. "Of course, it is possible to give more specifics. In ancient days, soothsayers predicted the future by studying the entrails of small animals, such as pigeons or squirrels. I have been trained in those methods."

A look of doubt crossed Lord Blakely's face. "You're going to slash open a bird?"

Jenny's heart flopped at the prospect. She could no more disembowel a dove than she could earn an honest living. But what she needed now was a good show to distract the marquess.

"I'll need to fetch the proper tools," she said.

Jenny turned and ducked through the gauzy black curtains that shielded the details of her mundane living quarters from her clients. A sack, fresh from this morning's shopping trip, sat on the tiny table in the back room. She picked it up and returned.

The two men watched her as she stepped back through a cloud of black cloth, her hands filled with burlap. She set the bag on the table before Ned.

"Ned," she said, "it is your future which is at stake. That means your hand must be the instrument of doom. The contents of that bag? You will eviscerate it."

Ned tilted his head and looked up. His liquid brown eyes pleaded with her.

Lord Blakely gaped. "You kept a small animal in a sack, just sitting about in the event it was needed? What kind of creature are you?"

Jenny raised one merciless eyebrow. "I was expecting the two of you." And when Ned still hesitated, she sighed. "Ned, have I ever led you astray?"

Jenny's admonition had the desired effect. Ned drew a deep breath and thrust his arm gingerly into the bag, his mouth puckered in distaste. The expression on his face flickered from queasy horror to confusion. From there, it flew headlong into outright bafflement. Shaking his head, he pulled his fist from the bag and turned his hand palm up.

For a long moment, the two men stared at the offending lump. It was brightly colored. It was round. It was—

"An orange?" Lord Blakely rubbed his forehead. "Not quite what I expected." He scribbled another notation.

"We live in enlightened times," Jenny murmured. "Now, you know what to do. Go ahead. Disembowel it."

Ned turned the fruit in his hand. "I didn't think oranges had bowels."

Jenny let that one pass without comment.

Lord Blakely fished in his coat pockets and came up with a polished silver penknife. It was embossed with laurel leaves. Naturally; even his pens were bedecked with proof of his nobility. His lordship had no doubt chosen the design to emphasize how far above mere commoners he stood. The marquess held the weapon out, as formally as if he were passing a sword.

Soberly, Ned accepted it. He placed the sacrificial citrus on the table in front of him, and then with one careful incision, eviscerated it. He speared deep into its heart, his hands steady, and then cut it to pieces. Jenny allotted herself one short moment of wistful sorrow for her after-dinner treat gone awry as the juice ran everywhere.

"Enough." She reached out and covered his hand mid-stab. "It's dead now," she explained gravely.

He pulled his hand away and nodded. Lord Blakely took back his knife and cleaned it with a handkerchief.

Jenny studied the corpse. It was orange. It was pulpy. It was going to be a mess to clean up. Most importantly, it gave her an excuse to sit and think of something mystical to say—the only reason for this exercise, really. Lord Blakely demanded particulars. But in Jenny's profession, specifics were the enemy.

"What do you see?" asked Ned, his voice hushed.

"I see…I see…an elephant."

"Elephant," Lord Blakely repeated, as he transcribed her words. "I hope that isn't the extent of your prediction. Unless, Ned, you plan to marry into the genus Loxodonta."

Ned blinked. "Loxo-wha?"

"Comprised, among others, of pachyderms."

Jenny ignored the byplay. "Ned, I am having difficulties forming the image of the woman you should marry in my mind. Tell me, how do you imagine your ideal woman?"

"Oh," Ned said without the least hesitation, "she's exactly like you. Except younger."

Jenny swallowed uncomfortably. "Whatever do you mean? She's clever? Witty?"

Ned scratched his chin in puzzlement. "No. I mean she's dependable and honest."

The mysterious smile slipped from Jenny's lips for the barest instant, and she looked at him in appalled and flattered horror. If this was how Ned assessed character, he would end up married to a street thief in no time at all.

Lord Blakely's hand froze above his paper. No doubt his thoughts mirrored hers.

"What?" Ned demanded. "What are you two staring at?"

"I," said Lord Blakely, "am dependable. *She* is—"

"You," retorted Ned, "are cold and calculating. I've known Madame Esmerelda for two full years. And in that time, she's become more like family than anyone else. So don't you dare talk about her in that tone of voice."

Jenny's vision blurred and her head swam. She had no experience with family; all she remembered was the unforgiving school where an unknown benefactor had paid her tuition. She'd known since she was a very small child that she stood alone against the world. That had brought her to this career—the sure knowledge that nobody would help her, and everyone would lie to her. Lying to them instead had only seemed fair play.

But with Ned's words, a quiet wistfulness filled her. Family seemed the opposite of this lonely life, where even her friends had been won by falsehoods.

Ned wasn't finished with his cousin. "You see me as some kind of tool, to be used when convenient. Well, I'm tired of it. Find your own wife. Get your own heirs. I'm not doing anything for you any longer."

Jenny blinked back tears and looked at Ned again. His familiar, youthful features were granite. Beneath his bravado, she knew he feared his elder cousin. And yet he'd stood up to the man just now. For her.

She wasn't Ned's family. She wasn't really his friend. And no matter what had transpired between them, she was still the fraud who bilked him of a few pounds in exchange for false platitudes. Now he was asking her to repay him with more lies.

Well. Jenny swallowed the lump of regret in her throat. If deceit was all she had, she would use it. But she hadn't saved Ned's life for his cousin's convenience.

Lord Blakely straightened. His outraged glower—that cold and stubborn set of his lip— indicated he thought Ned *was* a mere utensil. That

Lord Blakely was superior in intelligence and birth to everyone else in the room, and he would force their dim intellects to comprehend the fact.

He thought he was superior to his cousin? Well. She was going to make the marquess regret he'd ever asked for specifics.

"Ned, you recently received an invitation to a ball, did you not?"

He puckered his brow. "I did."

"What sort of a ball?"

"Some damned fool crush of a coming-out, I think. No intention of going."

The event sounded promising. There were sure to be many young women in attendance. Jenny could already taste her revenge on the tip of her tongue.

"You will go to this ball," she pronounced. And then she swept her arms wide, encompassing the two men. "You will both go to this ball."

Lord Blakely looked taken aback.

"I can see nothing of Ned's wife in the orange. But at precisely ten o'clock and thirty-nine minutes, Lord Blakely, *you* will see the woman you *will* marry. And you will marry her, if you approach her in the manner I prescribe."

The scrape of Lord Blakely's pencil echoed loudly in the reigning silence. When he finished, he set the utensil down carefully.

"You wanted a scientific test, my lord." Jenny placed her hands flat on the table in satisfaction. "You have one."

And if the ball was as crowded as such things usually were, he would see dozens of women in every glance. He'd never be able to track them all. She imagined him trying to scribble all the names in his notebook, being forced by his own scientific methods to visit every lady, in order to fairly eliminate each one. He would be incredibly annoyed. And he'd *never* be able to prove her wrong, because who could say he had recorded every woman?

Ned's mouth had fallen open. His hand slowly came up to hide a pleased smile. "There," he said. "Is that specific enough for you?"

The marquess pursed his lips. "By whose clock?"

One potential excuse slipped from Jenny's grasp. Not to worry; she had others.

"Your fob watch should do."

"I have two that I wear from time to time."

Jenny frowned. "But you inherited one from your father," she guessed.

Lord Blakely nodded. "I must say, that is incredibly specific. For scientific purposes, can you explain how you got all of this from an elephant?"

Jenny widened her eyes in false innocence. "Why, Lord Blakely. The same way I got an elephant from an orange. The spirits delivered the scene as an image into my mind."

He grimaced. She could not let her triumph show, and so she kept her expression as unchanging and mysterious as ever.

"So," Ned said, turning to his cousin, "you agree, then?"

Lord Blakely blinked. "Agree to what?"

"When you find the girl in question and fall in love, you'll agree Madame Esmerelda is not a charlatan."

The marquess blinked again. "I'm not going to fall in love." He spoke of that emotion in tones as wooden and unmoving as a dried-out horse trough.

"But if you did," Ned insisted.

"If I did," Lord Blakely said slowly, "I'd admit the question of her duplicity had not been scientifically proven."

Ned cackled. "For you, that's as good as an endorsement. That means, you'll consult Madame Esmerelda yourself and leave me be."

A longer pause. "Those are high stakes indeed. If this is to be a wager, what do you put up?"

"A thousand guineas," Ned said immediately.

Jenny nearly choked. She'd thought herself unspeakably wealthy for the four hundred pounds she'd managed to scrimp and save and stash away. A thousand pounds was more money than she could imagine, and Ned tossed it about as if it were an apple core.

Lord Blakely waved an annoyed hand. "Money," he said with a grimace. "What would either of us do with that paltry amount? No. You must risk something of real value. If you lose, you'll not consult Madame Esmerelda or any other fortune-teller again."

"Done," said Ned with a grin. "She's always right. I can't possibly lose."

Jenny couldn't bring herself to look at him. Because Ned could do nothing but lose. What if he began to doubt Jenny's long-ago assurances? What if he discovered that he owed his current happiness to the scant comfort of Jenny's invention? And Jenny could not help but add one last, desperately selfish caveat: What if Ned learned the truth and disavowed this curious relationship between them? He would leave her, and Jenny would be alone.

Again.

She inhaled slowly, hoping the cool air would help her calm down. The two men would go to the ball. Lord Blakely would look around. For all she knew, he might even decide to marry a girl he saw. And once he rejected all the women whose names he'd recorded, she'd tell him he'd seen a different woman at the appointed time out of the corner of his eye.

The wager would become a nullity, and she wouldn't have to see the fierce loyalty in Ned's eyes turn to contempt. Jenny's pulse slowed and her breath fell into an even rhythm.

Lord Blakely lounged back in his chair. "Something has just occurred to me."

The devilish gleam in his eye froze Jenny's blood. Whatever it was the dreadful man was about to say, she doubted he'd thought of it at that minute.

"What will stop her from claiming it was some other chit I was meant for? That I saw two girls at the designated time, and chose the wrong one?"

He'd seen through her. A chill prickled the ends of Jenny's fingers.

Ned frowned. "I don't know. I suppose if that happens, we'll have to call the bet off."

The marquess shook his head. "I have a better idea. Since Madame Esmerelda's seen everything in the orange, she'll be able to verify the girl's identity immediately."

He met her eyes and all Jenny's thoughts—her worries for Ned, the loneliness that clutched her gut—were laid bare in the intensity of his gaze.

His lip quirked sardonically. "We'll take her with us."

Want to read the rest of this book? You can buy Proof by Seduction *now.*

Other Books by Courtney

The Turner Series

Unveiled
Unlocked
Unclaimed
Unraveled

Not in any series

What Happened at Midnight
The Lady Always Wins

The Carhart Series

This Wicked Gift
Proof by Seduction
Trial by Desire

Acknowledgments

This novella, appearing in an anthology, originally had no space for acknowledgments. So here I am, five years later, finally acknowledging the people who helped me.

Tessa Dare, Carey Baldwin, and Franzeca Drouin were all extremely helpful.

The Northwest Pixies came through in my hour of need and read this novella on extremely short notice—Kris Kennedy, Darcy Burke, Tatia Talbot, and Rachel Grant all read this and discussed the ending, the middle, and the beginning. Without them, I would never have had any edits at all.

This was my first published work, and the response from readers was amazing. If you read *This Wicked Gift* in its original inception, and cared about it... Thank you so much. The beginning of an author's career is often the shakiest part. I would never have made it off the ground it without your enthusiasm. Thank you, thank you, thank you.

81838460R00093

Made in the USA
San Bernardino, CA
12 July 2018